The Daughter of Black Ice
-A Novel Written By-
Shameek A. Speight

D1522418

17

PA

Acknowledgements

Thank you to all my supporters that have been and continue riding with me all these years! It's been five years since I have published my first book, A Child of A Crackhead. A story I wrote to release the pain of my childhood, but I had no idea it would take a life of its own and become so big and so much more. I thank you all for that! It's my goal to be one of the best authors that touches the Earth, to be the King of Urban Horror, write books that most fear to touch, to entertain you, and give you nightmares! I promise to use my gift to paint a perfect picture with my words, to have you feel the pain of each character, to have you laugh and cry; my words will be a movie in your head. I hope you enjoy and Thank You so much for all the love. I Am the King of Urban Horror, and I'm only getting started.

Thank you to my team! My editor; La'shan Michele, thank you so much! Dextanie Henry, thank you for typing up my work. I know I'm a pain in the ass and the only person that still writes with pen and paper.

Thank you Tiffany Stephens, my tiff for always being on your job, my marketer and assistant. You take a lot of pressure off me. Thank you to my True Glory Team, my authors, and readers that stand by me no matter what and love my crazy mind.

Table of Contents

The Daughter of Black Ice

Written By:
National Best Selling Author
Shameek A. Speight

Chapter 1

"You are going to do what the fuck I tell you to do and I don't want to hear no more fucking lip!" Regina shouted, while swinging the broomstick. "Do you hear me, bitch? Can you fucking hear me?" Regina shouted, getting frustrated that Faith hasn't hollered out in pain yet.

Regina knew Faith wouldn't because she had been that way since she was a child. It was as if she was immune to pain and things of this world.

"Scream bitch! Scream!" Regina shouted, while Faith lay on the floor, curled up into a ball with her hands in a tight fist. She used her forearm to block her mother's powerful blows with the broomstick.

Faith knew there was no telling how far her mother would go on with beating her. For most of her life, her mother would beat her every day, until she broke a bone or Faith lost consciousness.

"Stop! I said stop!" Faith hollered in a deep dark tone that sent chills through Regina's body.

She froze in mid-swing and then, remembered who she was. "I'm your mother. Who the fuck you think you talking to? You think I'm scared of your ass?" Regina taunted.

Faith looked at her mother with an evil stare as if she wanted to chop her head off. Regina could feel her daughter's eyes piercing through her soul; a look and feeling she felt before and swore that she would never feel again.

Regina's fat, chubby arms shook as she reached her hand in between her double D breasts and removed a small chrome 380 handgun from under her shirt. She cocked it and aimed it at Faith's head.

"The day you try me will be the day I kill you. Your life is as worthless as a roach I step on and hear it crunch in my very own kitchen. Your life is as worthless as the trash I throw out into the garbage. You're just garbage! I regret the day you were born and I am waiting for the day for you to jump at me or try to leave me, so I can kill you! You're going to do what I tell you to do even if it means sleeping with a 100 men in a day, so fucking what. I'm going to get what you owe me and you owe me your life for bringing you into this fucking world!" Regina shouted, waiting for Faith to move funny, cough, or sneeze. Regina waited for any sudden movement or reason, so she could finally end her life. Regina stared at her daughter. Everything about her made her sick until her stomach twisted up in knots of disgust. All she could see was her father; there was no sign of herself in her.

Regina had the complexion of a peanut, standing at 5'6" tall. The many years of drinking and drugs had taken a toll on her body and face, which is now full of blemishes and dark spots with indentations, as if her skin was just deteriorating away. She once weighed 180 pounds with a voluptuous, thick, coke bottle shaped body, but that was years ago. Now, she's heavy set and weighs close to 300 pounds.

Regina continued to stare at her daughter and wanted to pull the trigger. Faith's chocolate skin complexion and almond shaped eyes made Regina's stomach bubble.

"Get your ass off the floor and sit on that bed!" Regina shouted, while still pointing the gun at Faith.

Faith looked at the dirty mattress that she called her bed. It had yellow and brown stains on it, but her mother refused to give her any bed sheets to cover the mattress.

"Bitch, don't you hear me calling you?" Regina shouted.

Faith slowly eased off the floor while trying not to show her mother that she was still in pain. After twenty years on this Earth, she knew of nothing her mother enjoyed more than getting high, except to see her in pain. It was as if the more she cried out, the more pain she inflicted upon her.

"Lift up your damn head," Regina ordered.

Faith looked at her mother as if she had lost her mind or the little bit that she had left in her. Her face tightened as she looked at the gun. *'If I fight, I know this bitch will kill me; but if I don't, there's no telling what she'll do to me or continue to do to me,'* Faith thought to herself. She took a deep breath, laid back and hitched up her long black dress, and fought the tears that were watering up in her eyes.

Regina looked over to the black dress that was lying next to the bed and smiled. She walked over to it, plugged in the curling iron and pulled out a glass pipe, no bigger than a cigarette. She stuffed one end with a large crack rock, the size of a small peanut, with her gun still aimed at her daughter's head. She pulled out a lighter from under her shirt that stayed resting in between her cleavage. That's where she kept most things hidden. She held the lighter to the end of the pipe and flicked the tip of it. The fire quickly cooked the crack. Regina inhaled deeply and held it, closing her eyes as if it was ecstasy, then slowly exhaled the thick, white crack smoke from her nostrils. She pulled hard on the glass pipe one more time, sucking in the rest of the thick white smoke. Regina could feel the glass pipe heat up. But from the many years of smoking crack and having her fingers burned, she could hardly feel anything. Most of her fingers had calluses from being burned. She placed the glass crack pipe on top of the dresser and picked up the now hot, curling iron.

"Open your mouth up, bitch!" Regina shouted.

"No mommy, no!" Faith pleaded, while crawling backwards, further up on the bed.

"Bitch, you think I'm playing with you! You must think this shit is a game," Regina said and swung, hitting Faith on the side of the head with the chrome 38 revolver.

"Ughh!" Faith groaned in pain as she felt like her head was almost knocked off her shoulders. She lay there, twisted up in pain as thoughts of attacking her mother went through her head. *'Fuck it, if she kills me. I don't have much to live for anyways. This can't be life.'*

"Bitch, you sit on your motherfucking ass and spread your legs!" Faith could hear her mother's voice shout.

The sound of it snapped her back into reality. She slowly opened her legs and her body began to tremble in fear as she tried to hide it from her mother, but it was too late. She could tell by the wicked smile on Regina's face that she was excited. Regina placed the hot curling iron on the inside of her thick legs.

"AHAHAH!" Faith hollered in pain and pulled her legs away, but not before the hot curling iron burnt through her flesh deeply. You could see the white meat and the smell of her cooked flesh lingered through the air, making the room smell like burnt popcorn. "Ahhhhh!" Faith continued to scream and holler, barely touching the burnt spot with her hand, in fear it would cause it to hurt more. A blow to her face gave her a newfound pain as Regina hit her with the handle of the gun. Faith could only see stars as

her world went black and she lost
consciousness.

Chapter 2

"Usshh!" Faith moaned in pain. Her hand was throbbing as if she had hit her hand with a sledgehammer repeatedly. She slowly opened her eyes while trying to gather her thoughts and remember what happened to her. She realized that she was in her room on her bed, laid out on her back, and was unable to move. She tried moving again, but she was stuck. She looked at her hands. "Oh God no! Oh God no!" she cried out loud, once she realized what her mother had done.

Her legs were spread wide open and tied down by ripped sheets to the bed frame and so were her hands. Faith could no longer fight back the tears as she had flashbacks of her mother tying her to the bed from the age of ten. She had different men come in to her room and do as they pleased to her; all so her mother could make some money to support her drug habit.

"I'm completely alone in this world. I have nobody. No family to count on to love and help me. God has turned his back on me from the moment I took my first breath. I really have nobody. Why lord? Why? What have I done for my mother to hate me so much? What have I done for me not to have a loving family? Why am I all alone with my pain, my struggles?" Faith asked out loud as she cried hysterically.

Regina burst through the door with a cigarette that was filled with crack. She took a deep pull, inhaling it in and then exhaling the smoke out of her nostrils.

"I see you up," she said with a wicked grin on her face. The sight of seeing her daughter in pain and feeling hopeless, brought joy to Regina. "Bitch, stop crying! You know the routine. I have three customers in line to pay you good money for your ass if they cum inside you. That's okay. Make them feel as if they're working with something, as if they got a big dick," Regina said and started laughing, staring back at her daughter. "Now, if you're fucking right, I will untie you. All you need to do is please these men and stop fighting them. You're too old for the shit you do. This keeps a roof over our heads and food in the house."

"Regina, fuck you! Fuck you! I can't believe I ever came out of you. I will always fight back. You have no idea what these men do to me or you don't care, saying this keeps the roof over our heads and food in the house. What food? There's never nothing for me to eat. You eat everything! If I dare try to cook something, you beat me with a baseball bat. This has nothing to do with providing for me or us. You're just sick and think that you can use my body forever to support your drug habit, but mother, I won't always be here. I'm twenty years old and one day, I'm going to leave you in this shitty small apartment by your damn self! What you going to do then? Huh? No one is going to pay for that fat, stinky, sweaty pussy then, huh? So, how will you take care of yourself then, bitch?" Faith asked while crying.

Regina's eyes opened up wide as a look of pure rage covered her face. Nothing hurt and cut deeper more than the truth. Her mind raced as she imagined her life without her daughter, her cash doll of a child. She knew she wouldn't survive at all without her.

"Oh, so you think you're going to run away with some prince charming and live happily ever after? Well baby girl, life doesn't work that way," Regina stated.

"I don't need any man to take care of me or anyone, for that matter. I'll finish school and work. The only reason I'm not in college is because you won't let me enroll, but every day the fear I have for you is beginning to die. The respect and love I have for you as my mother is gone, and the respect I have for you as a woman drowned in my tears as a little girl. You aren't shit and besides, why do you think a man wouldn't want to take me away, love me and take care of me? Don't they look right pass your washed up, fat self and pay you top dollar just for an hour inside me? Hahaha!" Faith said and started laughing. "You know how many guys want to marry me and take me out of here? Guess, mother, guess," Faith said with a scattered smile across her face.

"Oh bitch, you think I'm going to just let you leave me, huh? You think you'll make it in the real world without me, huh? You're a worthless piece of shit. I wish I fell down a flight of stairs while you were still in my stomach! I never wanted you, nor did your father!" Regina shouted back.

"Lies, lies, lies, all fucking lies. Why won't you tell me who my father is, mother? Who is the man you fear and hate so much, that every time you look at my dark skin complexion, you beat me? I know you fear him because you said I have his eyes and when I look at you, I see fear, mother. I can feel you're scared of me, deep down. It's like I can smell it in the air, like some kind of dog. I can sense all people's weaknesses for some reason, so mother, tell me why I can? Tell me who my father is and what he has done to make you hate me so much, mother," Faith said while fighting back her tears.

Her sarcastic ways seemed to all but vanish from the time she was able to speak. She had always asked about her father, but she had never gotten a straight answer from her mother. And no matter how bad her mother abused her, deep down, she loved Regina. She prayed that one day she would love her back, like a mother is supposed to love their child.

"You have a lot of mouth today, huh bitch? I got something for your ass," Regina smiled and looked at the bright red light on the curling iron that she plugged in and left on the nightstand. "Nice and hot," she mumbled to herself as she grabbed it off the black nightstand. "So, you went through a lot today? I got something for you, bitch," Regina said as she grabbed Faith's face with her left hand and squeezed it tightly, forcing her mouth wide open.

"Ughhh!" Faith groaned and struggled, but couldn't put up a fight against her mother.

Regina shoved the hot curling iron into her mouth, "Ughhh! Ughh!" Faith let out a muffle of screams and squirmed in excruciating pain.

The burning hot curling iron began to cook Faith's tongue and the meat on the inside of her cheeks. She could feel the skin bubble up and pop, as tears poured out from the corner of her eyes uncontrollably. She squirmed, twisting her head from side to side, but Regina had a tight, firm lock on her face, like a snake that tightens up its hold on its prey. The more the prey moved, the tighter the snake would squeeze until the prey completely stopped moving all together. The pain was excruciating and too much to bare.

"Mmmm! Mother stop! Please! Mmmm! Mother!" Faith tried to scream, but it sounded more like a muffled cry.

Her mother forced the hot curling iron deeper down her throat until she began to gag and choke. The heat and fumes made it impossible for her to breathe. Faith's eyes rolled to the back of her head as her body went into convulsions, shaking uncontrollably, and she lost consciousness.

"What the fuck!" Regina shouted, while watching her daughter's body shake as if she was having a seizure. "Oh, hell no bitch, you're not about to die on me! You're my fucking cash cow!" Regina yelled and tried pulling the curling iron out of Faith's mouth, but couldn't. The curling iron had burned the top of Faith's mouth, fusing the skin under it. It was now stuck, like burnt meat on aluminum foil that was left in the oven too long and almost impossible to peel away from the foil. Regina grabbed the curling iron with both hands and pulled with all her strength. "Ughhh!" she grunted and yanked it out. As soon as she did, Faith began to cough violently. Smoke came out of her mouth and a white foam mixed with blood gushed out of her mouth, dripping down her chin onto her chest. "Wake up bitch! You better not die on me!" Regina hollered and slapped Faith hard three times in the face, but got no response.

She stopped and studied her daughter, and saw that she was still breathing, but very slowly. "No man will ever want to keep you now," Regina said and pressed the curling iron against Faith's face on her right cheek, leaving a long deep burn mark across her face. She looked at her daughter in shock to see that she hadn't moved, flinched, or woke up yet. "Hmm, I hope this bitch isn't dead. The first of the month is next week and I need to make my rent money. I bet this will wake your ass up," Regina said as she spit on the curling iron. She bent over and moved Faith's panties to the side. She gently parted her daughter's pussy lips with her index finger and thumb, and with a wicked smile, she shoved the curling iron inside Faith's vagina. The shocking new pain that flowed through Faith had awakened her.

"Ahahahaha! Ahahahaha!" she hollered in excruciating pain as streams of tears poured out of her eyes and sizzled, like a hot plate from Applebee's. "Ahahaha!" she screamed, while squirming and turning. She used her vagina muscles to push out the curling iron. She could feel the inside of her vagina cooking. "Ahahaha!" Faith let out a scream that stopped Regina from pushing the curling iron even deeper.

Faith found the strength she never knew she had and pulled hard, ripping the sheets that strapped her hands in place. She sat up and head-butted her mother in her nose.

"Ughh," Regina groaned in pain and stumbled backwards, while trying to get her brain to readjust to what had just taken place. Before she knew it, Faith had pulled the curling iron out of her vagina and untied the white bed sheets off her ankles. She leaped off the bed, punching her mother in the face. "Ughh!" Regina screamed, while staring at her daughter, surprised with fear.

The look Faith had in her eyes was a look she had seen before; someone she prayed she would never see again. A right jab and a left hook made Regina's head move like one of those bobble head toys people keep on their desks.

"Ahhhhh!" Regina screamed with each blow.

Faith locked her hands on the back of Regina's neck and head-butted her three times. Then, using all her might, she kicked her knee, crashing into her mother's stomach.

"Noooo! Nooo!" Regina screamed, while falling to the ground. Her crying in pain was quickly silenced by Faith's bare feet kicking her in the mouth.

"Fuck this! I won't be a victim again," Faith mumbled as blood gushed out of Regina's now broken nose. The blood traveled down into Regina's mouth. She spit it out before she received a swift kick in the stomach. "I hate you! I hate you! All my life you think you can control me, hurt me, sell my body for money! Why? Why do you hate me? You're my mother!" Faith questioned Regina with rage in her voice and began to stomp Regina's thigh.

Regina reached her hand down her shirt, in between her double D cleavage, and dug around until she felt the handle of her chrome 380 handgun. She pulled it out from between her breasts and under her shirt quickly, as Faith continued to stomp on her thigh. She could feel it swelling up and a knot growing inside. In an awkward angle, she aimed. Before Regina could pull the trigger, Faith kicked the gun out of her hand, sending it a few feet across the room, next to the bathroom door.

"All my life I put up with your shit, but not anymore!" Faith screamed as she grabbed the curling iron off the floor.

"Noo! Lord no, help me," Regina cried out, while turning on to her stomach. She used her hands to try to help push herself up, but stumbled back on the wooden floor, from her legs being so sore.

"Oh, don't run now mother, let's finish what you started," Faith said. "No, no! You can't get away that easy," Faith said, while grabbing her mother's legs and dragging her backwards.

Regina's eyes opened in shock as her mind wondered how her 5'4" tall daughter, who only weighed 150 pounds, was able to pull her 300-pound frame, almost lifting her up off the floor. Regina's eyes opened wider as her daughter dropped her legs and grabbed her by her waist, popping the button off of her jeans. Next, she could feel Faith's small hands yanking off her jeans and panties.

"Nooo! Nooo!" Regina screamed and squirmed as she tried to get away as she felt her jeans now on her ankles. "I got to reach the gun. I must stop this little psycho bitch," Regina said to herself as her heart raced.

"Oh, you like to dish it out mother, but you can't take it. This is the last time that you will ever hurt me," Faith said while picking the hot curling iron back up.

A deep rage was in her eyes, but a twisted, wicked smile spread across her face, showing off her white teeth. She was looking at her mother with her jeans and panties down, hanging off of her ankles, while lying on her stomach. She looked like a large, blue whale that washed up onto the shore, wanting to be tossed back into the water, but was stuck.

"Squirming left to right was good for me, it'll be good for you too," Faith said.

"Ughh," Regina moaned in pain.

When she heard her daughter say those words, Regina stopped trying to sit up or crawl towards the bathroom door, which was where the gun was. "What the fuck you mean by that, you crazy bitch? I should have flushed you down the toilet the day you were born," Regina said. She turned her head to look behind her while smiling, knowing her words had hurt her daughter. She could tell by the way her eyes trembled that she was trying to fight back the tears. Regina's smile quickly disappeared when she noticed the hot curling iron in her daughter's hand. "What's good for me is good for you," Regina mumbled the words her daughter said. She screamed as reality sunk in that she was laying on the floor, damn near naked and helpless, and her daughter was about to do to her what she just did to her daughter. "Nooo! Nooo! Fucking Nooo!" Regina screamed and began to panic. She started to crawl for the front door, but Faith pulled her backwards and spread her legs.

"Like mother, like daughter, right mother?" Faith asked and aimed for her mother's fat vagina.

"Ussh!" Regina let out a grunting sound as she pushed the hot curling iron out of her vagina with her pussy muscles.

"It won't be that easy, bitch!" Faith shouted and pulled her mother by the legs, dragging her back some, and then rammed the hot curling iron back into her mother's vagina.

"Ahhhhh!" Regina hollered at the top of her lungs, as the sizzling sound of her pussy beginning to cook echoed through the room.

Tears poured down her eyes as she took deep breaths and remembered that she could handle this pain and take more. She had endured far worse pain by the hands of Faith's father. Regina tightened up her face and screamed; she gasped for air and could feel Faith pushing the hot curling iron deeper into her vagina. Her insides felt as if they were melting away. She closed her eyes, squeezing her eyelids tighter together, and then reopened them, focusing on the gun by the door. She used her fingernails to pull against the floor as her body crawled like a sneaky cat, and then, a smile spread across her face as her fingers became inches away from the chrome 380 handgun. She looked back to see if Faith was paying attention, but she was too consumed on inflicting pain. Regina reached with all her might and grabbed the revolver.

"Yes," she said while pulling back the chamber, making a bullet jump into the head of the gun. She pulled the gun close to her breast while laying flat on her stomach on the floor, knowing she had to wait until the right time before taking the shot.

"Hhmmm!" Faith groaned, getting frustrated that her mother had somehow learned to control the pain that she was inflicting on her. Faith pulled out the hot curling iron.

"Hmmm, I guess you can take pain better than I thought." Faith grabbed her mother by the legs and flipped her over.

Regina looked at her and squinted her eyes. "Better than you know. You have no idea what you are doing to me. You will never compare to the pain your father inflicted on me as a child!" Regina shouted, causing Faith to freeze in her tracks.

"Who is my father? Tell me about him. Tell me why you hate me so much," Faith inquired. The evil look in her eyes had disappeared. She stood there with the bloody curling iron in her hand with a look on her face, looking like an innocent child searching for answers.

"If you want to know who your father is, just look in the mirror, bitch. That's the only answer you will get from me before you die!" Regina screamed. She then raised the chrome 380 handgun that she had hidden with her hand, covering it over her breast. She aimed for Faith's forehead.

Faith knew this time it was over for her. All the years of abuse came down to this moment; the moment her mother had been waiting for. Finally, a reason to kill her. Faith squinted her eyes, watching the chrome revolver pointed at her head, and her mother's chubby finger slowly pulling back on the trigger. Faith's mind raced, knowing she didn't have any time to waste. She quickly tugged at the plug to the curling iron out of the socket and tossed the hot iron towards her mother's face.

"Ahhhhh!" Regina yelled, while squeezing the trigger and trying to duck from the curling iron's path.

The bullet jumped out of the 380 handgun, but not before Regina jerked her arm, causing her to miss her target. It missed the center of Faith's forehead by a few inches and slammed into the wall behind her. The steaming hot curling iron landed onto Regina's fat face.

"Ahahahahaha!" She hollered as it melted to the meat of her face.

Faith wasted no time and ran full speed, leaping over her mother and towards the bathroom door.

"Ugshh!" Regina hollered, while pulling the hot curling iron off of her face, ripping away pieces of burnt flesh. She stared at the large pieces of meat on the curling iron and screamed. "Ahahaha!" She took her hand and touched her right cheek to feel a deep hole in her face. Regina rolled back onto her stomach, stretched out her arms and gripped the 380 handgun with both hands.

Faith had made it to the front door. "Shit! Oh god! Oh God," she mumbled, while unlocking the third dead bolt, but the door had five dead bolts. She turned her head back and could see her mother aiming at her. **Boom! Boom! Boom!**

The 380 handgun sent three bullets flying towards Faith. The first bullet slammed into the back of her shoulder, ripped out through the front of her chest and slammed into the metal front door. The second bullet ripped through the meat of her back and came out through her stomach, sending chunks of flesh onto the door. The third bullet hit the back of her thigh and got lodged there.

"Ahhahaha!" Faith screamed as her leg went back and she caught herself before she hit the ground. She used all of her energy to unlock the two remaining locks as fast as she could.

"Oh, no you don't bitch!" Regina shouted, while watching her daughter open the front door. She squeezed the trigger four more times, sending bullets flying.

Faith hit the floor and the bullet flew passed her head. She jumped up and hopped on one leg, doing her best to run, knowing that it was only a matter of time her mother found the strength to sit up and chase her to finish the job. She ran down the hallway, leaving a trail of blood. She reached the steps and regretted that she lived on the third floor. "Ahhhh! Ushh!" She groaned and cried, while leaking down each step.

Regina pulled up her panties and ran into her bedroom and dug under her pillow, where she had an extra clip for the handgun. She pressed a button and released the chamber. Taking the empty clip out and putting in the new one, she put a bullet in the gun. "Ahahaha! Shit!" Regina groaned while trying to walk, but the soreness inside her pussy was causing her to scream. "Fuck! Fuck! You little bitch! Ahhhhh! I'll make sure you're dead!" Regina shouted, hoping to see her daughter's body squirming in the hallway. "Shhhhh!" She let out a hissing sound with every step she took. She smiled when she made it to the front door and saw a pool of thick, red blood. "Damn, I hit that bitch good. I will see my dead daughter soon."

She walked out of the apartment, inching every step. Her facial expression changed to panic when she noticed the blood trail hadn't stopped in the apartment building, but kept going down the staircase. She could see Faith on the final flight of stairs before she reached the lobby. She aimed the handgun and fired wildly below toward Faith's body.

"Noo! Noo! Die, die! Noo! I will not live in fear, not again. You won't scare me like your father. Fuck you! Fuck you, Black Ice!"

Faith could hear her mother scream out over the loud gunshots that echoed through the stairway. Knowing she couldn't take another bullet, Faith sucked up all the pain running through her body as she could. She ran across the building lobby and out of the front door.

"What the fuck!" She could see two young thugs having sex, sitting on a parked car. Faith held her stomach tightly as blood poured out of it and down her legs.

"I can't, she'll get me. I can't stop," she mumbled, repeating herself, knowing that it wouldn't take her mother too long to reach her.

"Oh my God! Call the ambulance!" a woman in her mid-thirties called out as she got off the bus coming from work. She looked around and wondered why nobody was helping Faith, but then again, this was Staten Island. People mind their business out here. Just last week, a man beat his girlfriend to death in front of their building and nobody helped. "Sweetie, you must stop moving. Stay still and lay on the floor while I call the cops. Who did this to you?" the beautiful, brown skinned woman asked.

Faith turned her head and looked at her for the first time. She had short hair that was cut in a bob hairstyle, her eyes were a beautiful light brown and she was thick, not fat, but she had a little stomach.

"I can't stop. I just can't stop! I must keep moving," Faith said, while moving. Faith moved down the block, turning the corner.

The brown skinned woman that was by her side continued to race after her in a rapid speed.

"Ugh, I don't feel so well," she groaned and held the lady's shoulders as she stumbled and tried to catch her, but she hit the sidewalk hard.

"Oh my God, sweetie, please stay still and keep your eyes open, don't go to sleep," the woman ordered, while kneeling down next to Faith, on her cell phone calling the police.

"I can't keep my eyes open," Faith mumbled as she felt herself becoming groggy.

A black van pulled up next to them, stopping short, causing the tires to make a squealing sound. Faith's eyes opened wide as a dark skinned, bald headed man with a black leather pea coat stepped out of the back of the van. He was tall and muscular with a scar on his face. Faith knew right away that something wasn't right with the man. He walked up to them and was now standing behind the brown skinned woman, who hadn't noticed him because she was too busy focusing on Faith.

"Run! Run!" Faith panicked, but it came out as a whisper as she coughed up blood.

"Shhhhh, honey don't talk, you need to save your energy. The ambulance should be here any second. God, please send them faster," the brown skinned woman mumbled.

Faith looked at the woman and wondered how this complete stranger could care more about her than her mother did. Faith closed her eyes then opened them, realizing that the dark skinned man was still standing there. In one swift move, Black Ice pulled out one of his chrome bulldog revolvers and swung.

"Ughh! Ughh!" the woman screamed from the new throbbing pain she felt on the back of her head. She turned around to see what had just hit her and realized it was a mistake.

Black Ice grinned and swung once more, hitting the woman in the temple on the left side of her head.

"Ahhhhh!" She let out a weak scream before passing out.

Two henchmen, dressed in all black, hopped out of the van. "What do you want us to do boss?"

"Grab them both and put them in the van. Be very careful with the dark skinned one. If you're not, I'll cut your fucking balls off, and burn the whole so you don't bleed to death. And while you lay there naked, crying like little bitches, I'll force you to watch one of my dogs eat your nut sack and chew on it as if it were bubble gum. Then order him to finish you off," Black Ice said through clenched teeth.

The henchmen lowered their heads in fear. "Yes boss," one henchman replied.

"Don't 'yes boss' me, hurry up and get her in the van before she bleeds to death!" Black Ice ordered. The two henchmen swiftly picked both of the women up and hopped in the back of the van. Black Ice jumped into the driver's seat and started up the van.

Regina limped as fast as she could out of the lobby. She looked at the gun in her hand and smiled. "I got you now, little bitch. I'll do to you what I should have done to your father years ago," she mumbled to herself, while following the thick trail of blood.

She followed it down the block, turned the corner and stopped suddenly in her tracks. Her heart pounded hard in her chest, feeling as if it was going to burst. "No! Nooo! Nooo! Noooooo!" she screamed, while watching the black van pull off, but not before she made eye contact with Black Ice through the driver's side mirror.

He grinned and lip-synced the words, "I'll be back for you, bitch."

"Ahhhhh!" Regina screamed and took off running in the opposite direction.

Chapter 3

"Ughhh! Uhhh!" Faith groaned in pain. She forced her eyes to open and could now see a handsome, muscular, dark skinned man, standing over her with his head tilted to the side, as if he was examining her. "Who are you and where am I?" she asked as her throat was sore. She stared at the man. Everything about him seemed so familiar, but she didn't know how because she had never even seen him before. There was something terribly wrong with him, she could sense it. Her body was telling her to run. "Who are you?" Faith asked again as she awoke even more. She could hear what sounded like a woman, screaming and hollering in pain in the background.

"You haven't earned that answer yet. You have to show me way more before I can claim you as one of mines," Black Ice said in a deep tone.

Faith closed her eyes for a second and when she had opened them again, her whole facial expression had changed. The woman that stopped and helped her was now standing naked in front of her with her, makeup running down her face from crying. Faith looked at her closely. She looked like a former image of herself and could feel the pain written all over her face. Her perfect dark brown skin was completely covered in black and dark red bruises.

"This is Brandy. You met her the night she stopped and helped you. I know she wished she would have never stopped and helped you now, don't you?" Black Ice asked and then, yanked her by her head and slowly let his tongue travel on her neck.

Faith could feel the drugs running through her system that kept her feeling dizzy. She tried to fight it so she could figure out what the hell was going on. She tried to sit up but she couldn't. She lifted her head and could see she was naked with a thick, long bandage wrapped around her stomach, completely covering it, and her legs were wrapped up. She looked around to see that she was in a very large, luxury bedroom, the size of two apartments. Across the room, she noticed another woman in her mid-thirties, shaking and standing naked. She was of light skinned complexion.

"Come over here, now," Black Ice ordered in a demanding tone. The woman inched her way towards him. "Both of you stand in front of her now."

Brandy and the next woman stood in front of Faith's bed. Black Ice grinned while placing a five inch, double bladed, razor sharp knife on the bed.

"What's that for?" Faith asked in a weak tone.

Black Ice smiled, showing off his set of perfect white teeth. He pulled a pack of Newport cigarettes out of his pocket and pulled one of them out of the box. Then he pulled out a small Ziploc bag that was the size of someone's finger, filled with small crack rocks. Faith's eyes grew wide because she had seen this same routine done before, many times, but only by one person, which was her mother. He stuffed the crack rock into the cigarette, pulled the lighter out of his pocket and lit the cigarette. The crack rock sparked up as he inhaled deeply, holding in the smoke, and then exhaling through his nostrils. The white part of his eyes turned dark red. Everything in Faith's mind told her that she should fear this man, but for some reason, she didn't.

Who was he? Why does he feel so familiar and why is my mother the only person that smoked her cigarette mixed with crack like this man? If he smokes that stuff, could I be related to him in some type of way? Could he be my father? But how? Where has he been all my life? A million thoughts ran through Faith's mind.

The smell of crack lingered in the air. The screams of other women were getting louder, coming from outside of the steel bedroom door. Black Ice moved closer to the bed, exhaling one more smoke out of his nose.

"All those questions you have been asking yourself your whole life, I'll answer them. I'll tell you who you really are and why your mother hates you so much," Black Ice stated.

"Really?" Faith replied, not believing her ears. All her life she felt empty, not knowing why her mother hated her.

"Yes really, but there's one catch. You must take the knife and pick one of these nice ladies, and then cut out something they really need or are going to miss very badly. If you'll do that, I'll tell you everything," he bargained, while squinting his eyes at her as if he was looking at her soul.

"Wait. What?" Faith asked.

"You heard me child. It's not hard at all, just let your anger out. I promise you, you will enjoy it. You choose between the two of them. You can pick Brandy, whose only mistake was being nosey and trying to help you, or Nakia. I know if I had to choose one, it would be Brandy, just to see the sweet look of betrayal on her face," Black Ice said and busted out laughing. "HAHAHA!" His laugh was dark and creepy, so it sent a funny sense through their bodies, causing their stomachs to bubble up.

"What do you mean, cut out a body part?" Faith asked.

Black Ice's face twisted up and he tilted his head to the side and gave her a look that said, 'Bitch really, you're just testing my patience and this isn't a test for me, but a test for you to see if you're ready for the knowledge I will teach you.'

"You're not going to like me being pissed the fuck off," Black Ice said through clenched teeth.

Faith picked up the knife and looked at Brandy and Nakia, standing on the side of the nightstand of the bed. "Why the fuck y'all don't run and get the fuck out of here?" Faith whispered.

"You have no idea where we are and who that man is, do you? There is no running or escaping, compared to what the outside of this bedroom is like. You'll wish for death. I watched him feed women to animals and his men gang rape women. We're all dead, sooner or later. It's just a matter of time," Brandy whispered back.

Faith looked at both of the women with a confused look, but then remembered, it took her years to finally fight back the abuse that her mother put her through.

Both women stood there trembling in fear, looking like night and day. Brandy was a thick, brown skinned woman with a little gut. Other than that, she was drop dead gorgeous with curly Brazilian weave in her head that stopped at her shoulders. Nakia was slim built and had to weigh no more than 120 pounds. She had double D sized breasts that looked like huge, honey melons. She had a beautiful smooth, clear skin complexion. Her hair was a mess as if she hadn't used a comb or brush in months.

Faith continued to look at both women, and then behind them was Black Ice. "I can't do what you're asking. That's too much. These women haven't done anything to me. Shit, if anything, Brandy helped save my life! Why the fuck would I want too-"

Before Faith could finish her sentence, Black Ice stepped in between the two women. For a 6'2" tall man that weighed 230 pounds of pure muscle, he moved like a cat, fast and swift. He swung with only half his might, punching Faith in the jaw.

"Ughhh!" Faith seen stars and tried to keep from choking on her own tongue. The blow was so strong that she said a few words that made no sense at all.

"Bitch, I gave you the opportunity of a lifetime to know who you really are. I felt that was too soft," he said, while grabbing her wrist and twisting it until the knife dropped out of her hand. Black Ice grinned, seeing she didn't scream out in pain like a normal person.

"Get off her; leave her alone!" Brandy shouted and hopped on his back. Her 160-pound body frame caused him to stumble forward for a second, losing his balance, but his strong thigh locked in place. He bent over, tossing Brandy over his shoulder.

"Ahhhhh!" she screamed as she hit the wooden floor so hard, it knocked the wind out of her.

"No! No! Don't hurt her!" Faith pled and tried to ease off the bed, but couldn't, forgetting for a minute that she was badly hurt.

"I asked you to do one simple fucking thing, child, and you froze the hell up like a punk! It was so easy. Let me show you," Black Ice said and picked up the knife.

Nakia seen the look in his eyes and took off running. "Noo! Noo!" She ran towards the bedroom door, knowing getting eaten alive could be better than anything Black Ice had in his plans for her. "Ughh ahh!" she screamed as Black Ice swiftly kicked her, knocking her off her feet.

"Now, where the fuck you think you going, bitch? I have a lesson to teach the child and guess what? I choose you to demonstrate on."

"Noo! Ughh no!" Nakia cried out, her tears now soaking the wooden floor. She felt Black Ice's huge hands grab her ankles. Knowing he had her in his grips caused Nakia to act a damn fool, screaming even harder and wiggling around. "Noo! Noo! Ahhh! No, help me! Help me, please!"

Faith tried hard, but was unable to move. Whatever drug Black Ice had her on caused her body to become numb. The pain was starting to wear off. Her stomach cramped up and her shoulder ached like a pain she never felt before. Brandy stood on the floor freezing, unable to move, while screaming.

"Ahhhh!" Nakia screamed, while being dragged to the next side of the large room. She felt a rope being wrapped tightly around both her legs, and then felt her body elevate.

Black Ice had a rope running through one of the metal beams in the ceiling. As he pulled the rope, he lifted Nakia off the ground and up into the air. In three strong pulls, Nakia was now hanging upside down in the air, five feet high, dangling around. Black Ice grabbed her chin, causing her body to stop spinning around. "When I said take a body part, I mean that. It's so very simple, child," he said in a dark tone and leaned in to kiss Nakia.

Fear was written all over her face as own tears blinded her, from too much water in her eyes. She took her lips in so he couldn't kiss her.

"Hmm," Black Ice grinned, showing off his perfect smile. "Hahahaha! You bitch need a little attention and she don't know how to act," he said, and then squeezed her cheeks so hard, Nakia could feel her teeth cracking and the taste of blood in her mouth.

"Ughh! Ahhh! No! No!" she managed to say. Just as her lips poked back out, Black Ice grabbed her bottom lip and pulled it out, stretching it. "Umm! Ummm!" Nakia screamed, trying to squirm free from the ropes. She reached for his face and tried to claw out his eyeballs, but he just knocked her hands down as if she was a child reaching for a toy.

"You do it like this," he said, while keeping his eyes on Faith across the room on the bed. In one swift move, he swung his right hand that held the double bladed knife and sliced off Nakia's bottom lip. Before Nakia could react from what just happened and scream in pain, he grabbed her top lip and sliced it off.

"Ahhhhhhhhhhh!   Assh!" Nakia hollered in excruciating pain, while choking on her own blood. "Ahhh!"   She continued to scream and wiggle to get free. She tried to do a sit up so she could reach the rope on her ankles, but she never been to a gym in her twenty-nine years on earth, so doing a sit up was impossible, especially upside down. *'Shit, why would I need to go to the gym or do a sit up? I never gain weight, I will stay this perfect size for life,'* Nakia used to tell herself every day. But for the first time in her life, she wished that things were different.

Black Ice smiled like the cat that swallowed the canary, while looking at the fact that Nakia didn't have lips, and it made it look like she was smiling. All you could see was her teeth and gums, covered in dark red blood. Nakia looked up and could see her lips on the floor. She watched

Black Ice's brown Timberland boots, slowly stepping on them, squirting blood and the insides in all directions to flatten and completely dry them. "Hahahahaha!"

Nakia, Brandy and Faith knew he wasn't human and that he was something else evil. He grabbed Nakia's left arm. She tried to yank it away, but there was no use. Black Ice looked at Faith. "If you want to know who you are, watch. This is who you are; you are me. If not, then you are her. Pick one child. Do you want to be the predator or the prey, to be helpless or to be the monster? There's only two people in the world, you're either the sheep or the wolf. You can't be both, baby, so sooner or later, you're going to have to pick one. And trust me child, it's in your nature to be a wolf," Black Ice said and grabbed Nakia's side of her breast, squeezing it. "Hmm, it looks like a giant Kiss candy bar," Black Ice said and began to laugh, while gripping it even tighter. He raised his right hand that held the knife and began to slice sideways on her breast as if he was slicing up a tomato in halves.

"AHAHAH! Nooo!" Nakia screamed as the sharp knife cut through her flesh. Blood oozed out of the new wounds from her breast, dripped down her neck and into her face, and then into her mouth. "UGHH USHH!" Nakia spit out the fat, trying her best not to choke on her own blood. "Ahhhh!" She continued to scream in excruciating pain while squirming around. She prayed that she would become free.

"Shut up bitch, you're screaming way too fucking much!" Black Ice hollered through gritted teeth, losing his patience from the sound of her voice. He plugged the knife deep inside of her.

"Ughh! Ahhhh!" Nakia gasped for air when she felt the knife deep inside of her. She could feel that it pierced her, just below her stomach.

Faith's eyes opened wide in disbelief. She covered her mouth with her left hand to keep from screaming. *'What the fuck! Who is this man and why is he doing this?'* Faith thought.

Brandy stood naked on the floor, crying hysterically, "This is only a dream. This can't be real because things like this don't happen in real life."

Black Ice turned his head and looked at both of them. *'He's enjoying this. I can't believe this sick fucker is enjoying this shit,'* she thought to herself.

Black Ice gripped the handle of the knife that was jammed deep in Nakia's lower stomach, piercing her bladder. She tried to scream, but she couldn't catch her breath. Something was keeping her from breathing right. She gasped for air as her tears dripped out her eyes and traveled down her forehead on to the wooden floor.

Black Ice's face grinned while pulling down the knife, the sharp razor blade that ripped her insides. Black Ice licked his lips as he continued to pull down, tearing open her stomach.

Nakia's body shook back and forth, like a fish out of water, as he pulled the knife all the way down to her chest and yanked it out. Faith and Brandy's eyes popped wide open in fear and disbelief.

"How the fuck is she still alive?" Faith asked out loud.

Black Ice looked towards her with a psycho look on his face. "You'd be surprised, child, how much pain the human can stand. It fights to stay alive and will continue to do so until the mind and the soul gives up," Black Ice said. While looking at the long sliced wound he made, he stuck his fingers into the wound and forced it open.

For the first time in minutes, Nakia was able to catch her breath and let out a piercing scream, "AAAHHHHHH!" She hollered at the top of her lungs. It was the last sound she ever made as her internal organs gushed out of her body, hit her in the face, and then hit the floor, looking like a pile of steaming raw meat. Her body bucked for a few more seconds then stopped, as she died with her eyes open, staring at Faith and Brandy.

"OH GOD!" Brandy repeated while sitting on the floor, holding herself and rocking back and forth. "This can't be real, this can't be real," she said, and then covered her mouth, as she felt the vomit travel from her stomach to her throat and out of her mouth. She tried to swallow it and push it back down but couldn't. The vomit pushed its way up out her mouth and through her fingers as she tried to cover her mouth. "USSH! UGH!" She coughed a few times as vomit came out of her nostrils.

"You nasty little bitch, you're going to clean that up!" Black Ice shouted and then walked over to Faith, whose mind was still trying to register all what she witnessed.

'What the hell was going on?' She stared at Nakia, hanging upside down by her feet, gutted like a pig, with all her insides now on the floor in a pool of blood. "Huh!" Faith said, surprised how fast and quick Black Ice could move.

He was now standing in front of her with a rag in his hand. "You're not ready yet, I'll know when you are and then, I'll come for you," he said. He then put the rag over her mouth and nose.

"MMMM! STOP! STOP! What are you doing?" Faith screamed, but it came out muffled. She tried to fight but was still too weak from her injuries. She smelled something funny on the rag, something sweet, as her eyes became heavy from inhaling the chemical. Soon, she was lying back down on the bed and unable to fight her sleep.

He removed the rag from her mouth and nose. "Who are you?" She managed to whisper.

He bent over and spoke into her ear in a low tone, "I am your father!" This was the last thing she heard before she lost consciousness.

Chapter 4

Faith felt a small sharp pain in her hand. "Get off of me! Get off of me!" she shouted while swinging. She felt his fists crash into her soft face.

"Help! Help!" a woman screamed in pain while panicking.

The sound of her voice caused Faith to open her eyes, while she was swinging wildly. The first thing she noticed was that she was in a completely different room. In the room she was in before, the walls were white. Faith stopped swinging to look at the lady in the pink nurse uniform, running towards the door with her right eye, screaming for help.

"Help me!" She opened the room door and ran out.

Not a second later, a dark-skinned, heavy set man appeared, dressed in a green scrub uniform, along with a short, heavy set brown-skinned woman in the pink scrubs, still holding her eye.

"Where is he? Did he send you? Where am I?" Faith shouted, balling up her fists. She then realized an IV was in her hand and put both her hands up, preparing to fight. She ripped the IV needle out of her hand real fast, looking for any object she could use as a weapon. *'That big fucker not about to cut me open like Black Ice did Nakia. Hell fucking no,'* Faith thought to herself as the dark-skinned, heavy set man stood by the door way with the lady in the pink scrubs, still holding her eye.

Just then, another person had entered the room. "Hmmm," Faith let out a soft moan without knowing it, as her defense lowered. She had never seen such a fine, handsome young man in her life.

"Miss, please calm down, we're here to help you. You are at Jamaican Hospital in Queens. I'm Doctor Monroe and you've been terribly injured, shot twice and burned all over your body. It looks like someone worked on you before you got here, removing one of the bullets that was stuck in you and stopped your bleeding, then dropped you off at the emergency room front doors. Do you remember anything miss?"

"Huh," Faith said. The sound of his voice had put her in a trance. She had forgotten where she was and that she was staring, but she couldn't help it.

Doctor Monroe was 5'11" with a wide, stocky frame, like he worked out every other day. He had a brown skinned complexion with a low fade haircut that connected to his goatee. He was, by far, the most handsome man Faith had ever laid eyes on. He looks almost as if he belongs on TV.

"Miss, do you remember anything? Can you recall what happened to you?" The sound of his voice snapped her back into reality.

"Huh," she replied. *'How do I tell him my mother abused me my whole life and pimped me out to dirty old men for drugs and money, and then she tried to kill me when I tried to fight back? Or better yet, should I tell him about the guy who claimed he was my father that gutted a woman alive in front of my face like a pig? Umm, I think it will be better if I just keep this to myself,'* Faith thought to herself. "Umm, I can't remember anything. I just remember walking down the street, and then feeling a sharp pain and blacking out," Faith said while holding her head.

"It's okay miss, I can tell you have been through a lot. I'm not going to rush you into remembering something terrible. Do you remember your name?" Doctor Monroe asked.

"Yes, my name is Faith," she replied, while removing her hand from her forehead.

Doctor Monroe now stood in front of her. Faith tried not to moan when she smelled his cologne lingering in the air, as he walked through the room. "Look up at me and let me see your eyes," Dr. Monroe stated while pulling out a small flash light, the size of a pen, from his front white coat pocket. He shined the light in her eyes. "Wow!" he mumbled.

"What? What is it, is something wrong?" Faith asked nervously, wondering what else could be wrong with her, as if being shot and burnt wasn't enough.

"Nothing is wrong, Faith. It's just that I have never seen eyes like yours on a dark skinned woman in years," Doctor Monroe replied, knowing her eyes were truly one of a kind.

Her eyes were something she had grown to hate her whole life, because she got them from her mother and the men that raped her would want her to keep her eyes open during sex.

"No, I mean nothing by it, Miss, your eyes are just beautiful," Doctor Monroe replied, and then looked at her face for the first time. When he had first entered, he had seen her but she wasn't conscious, so he never really looked at her, only as a patient. Her light brown eyes made her chocolate skin glow. She was beautiful, even with a burn scar across her left cheek. Doctor Monroe smiled, touching her skin. "Who are you?" he asked in a low deep tone, fascinated by her.

"That's a question that I'm still trying to figure out myself," Faith replied, taking his hand into hers.

"Umm, be careful, Doctor. She has a mean left hook," the nurse in the pink scrubs said.

Her voice caused Faith and Doctor Monroe to break their embrace, pulling their hands away from each other. Faith looked behind the Doctor to see the nurse giving her a stink look. Faith raised her left eyebrow and smirked.

'This bitch has no idea who she is dealing with but now isn't the time,' Faith thought to herself.

Doctor Monroe wrote something down on her chart. "I need for you to rest, Faith. I'll be back to check on you later on today, and Bria, here, is your night nurse. Anything you need, she will handle," Dr. Monroe said with a seductive smile. Then he turned around and left the room.

Chapter 5

For the next two weeks, Dr. Monroe and Faith had become extremely close. He would come in her room every night for hours and talk to her, trying to get inside her mind.

"Well, you're healing up pretty good. In a few days, you'll be able to leave here," Dr. Monroe said, while checking her wounds and rewrapping them.

"What if I don't want to leave here? What if I'll miss our conversations too much?"

"Well, there's other ways you can have all my attention," Faith's doctor replied.

"Oh really and how is that?" Faith replied, showing off her pretty white teeth.

He gently touched her face then pulled her in closer. Their lips met as they slowly kissed. As their lips parted, their tongues danced in each other's mouths. His hands traveled around her body then firmly squeezed her breast. She let out a soft moan,

"Mmm," his lips traveled from her chin down to her neck while pulling out her right breast; which resembled a Hershey Kiss.

He wondered if it taste as good as it looked as he gently placed his lips onto her nipple, "Umm," he groaned while listening to her soft moans.

"Mmmm," Faith let out a soft moan, while feeling her pussy throb and getting wet. *'God, I just want him inside of me right now,'* she thought to herself and grabbed his thick dick through his black pants.

"I want you," he groaned, letting go of her breast while pulling her back.

Faith held her head down. "I'm not what you think I am. I don't even have a place to stay when I get discharged from the hospital. I'm not a Barbie doll; my life is more like a nightmare that you wish was a dream. I feel like you have been the closest I had to a dream. I feel like I don't deserve you," Faith said, while her mind replayed her mother's words before she shoved the hot curling iron into her. *'No man will ever want you, your worthless, nothing but a dirty hoe.'* "I'm not good," Faith stated.

"Shhhhh, don't talk like that, you deserve the world and even more than that. I look into your eyes and I can see a woman whose never been loved properly. It's going to be my job to show you how a man is supposed to take care of you," Dr. Monroe stated.

"Dr. Monroe, how could you feel this way, considering you have only known me for a short amount of time?" Faith asked.

"Stop it. I told you about calling me, Dr. Monroe, just call me by my first name, Antonio. And like I said, everything I need to know about you, I can see in your eyes. I can feel it. Now, I hear what you are saying about not having a place to live, but I can fix that. I know this is a little forward, but I want for you to stay with me at my condo in Queens. I'm barely there, I'm always here working and I barely use it. Like I told you, I have a few homes. When you're ready to talk about your past, you can," Antonio stated.

"But-" Faith started to speak, but he kissed her deeply, stopping her from speaking.

He dug inside the white lab coat and pulled out a key, a cell phone, and a credit card in his hand. "You'll be discharged tomorrow. I'll be working. So, use the card to buy you some clothes and take a cab to the condo. I'll meet you there later on," Antonio stated.

"Wait, wait, this is too much, too soon," Faith replied.

"It's never too much or too soon, you don't have a place to lay your head. Now you do. You don't have family that can come and help you, now you do. We'll discuss this tomorrow," Dr. Monroe said and then walked away, leaving the room.

Faith sat on the bed in the green hospital gown, staring at the phone, credit card, and the keys. "This can't be real."

She heard the room door open and quickly put the items under her pillow. She looked to see the nurse, Erika, enter the room with her face twisted up in disgust, looking at Faith as if she was a piece of shit she stepped on the sidewalk. "You can fix your face and stop looking at me like that," Faith said, not knowing what Erika had against her. It wasn't as if she was ugly. Erika was in her mid-twenties, short, overweight, brown skinned with a beautiful face. "For two weeks, you've been giving me that stank face, even after I apologized for hitting you. What problem you have with me?" Faith asked, while Nurse Erika straightened up the room and checked the monitors.

She stopped what she was doing and just stared at Faith before speaking. "I'm just tired of hoes like you winning. You bitches get to travel all around the world while real women, like me, still got to work twelve hours a day and still don't come up in life. You hoes just look cute, post ass pictures on social media, suck every dick that comes in your face, and end up getting married to the rich man after you done fucked three football teams worth of men," Erika said while rolling her neck.

Faith looked at her with a confused facial expression. "Like, I don't know what your problem is or what the hell you talking about. Antonio, I mean, Dr. Monroe is nothing more than my friend. I could see that you want him, but sweetie, if he wanted you, you'd have him. You work with him every day. So, you mad because he's more attracted to me, a woman he just met? You mad that he treats me better than any man that has ever entered your life? I'm not to blame for your fucked up love life. The real problem is that you mad at me because I have edges, walls, and manners, and your bum ass standing here missing all three. Bitch, you keep coming at me like that, the next time I'll punch your ass in the face, and it won't be by accident," Faith said with her teeth clenched. You could feel her anger rising, the same anger she felt when she tried to kill her mother. Faith lowered her head. "Breathe, calm down," she mumbled to herself.

"Yea, I'd like to see you try it. You caught me off guard the first time. So trust, that shit won't happen again," Erika said while looking at Faith, sizing her up and down, knowing she had a hundred pounds over her. All she had to do was grab her, get her on the ground and sit on her chest while punching her in the face. The thought of it played over and over in her head, causing a huge grin on her face. "You think you're special, it's only a matter of time before Dr. Monroe sees right through that. You hoes stay winning, but niggas get tired of that pretty face and used pussy, very fast. Here's a little rule I learned from my mother. Never trust a nigga that suck your titties and don't tuck them back in your bra. That nigga gone always leave you hanging." Looking down at Faith's breast, she said sarcastically, "Your left breast is out, boo boo." And walked out of the room with a stupid smirk on her face.

Faith looked down and quickly tucked her breast back in her bra under her gown. "Oooh, I hate that bitch. I should gut her fat ass like a pig," Faith blurted. "No, that's not me, that's not who I am." She calmed herself as she repeated the words over and over.

"And who the fuck you think you are?" Faith heard a low, deep voice say. The sound of it gave her goosebumps and the hair on the back of her head stood up. She lifted her head up to see Black Ice standing in the doorway, covered in a brown trench coat. She started to open her mouth to scream. "Now, you're really going to scream like a little punk? If you do that shit, I'll be so disappointed in you that I'll chop your motherfucking head off right here, and play soccer with it for three days before I kick it in the sewer, where it belongs," Black Ice threatened, meaning every word. Faith held her scream in, knowing he was serious. "So, who are you? I bet your slow ass still doesn't know. You think you're like them?" he said pointing at the door. "You're nothing like them, princess. You're a fucking killer and don't even know it, but you will. You'll see that you don't belong in their world, following their pussy ass rules. You're my child and you're above that. These people are sheep, we are wolves."

"You, you are my father?" Faith asked, stuttering over her words, "Where have you been my whole life?" she asked with a confused look on her face.

"I told you little bitch, you haven't earned the right to ask me any questions yet. I just came to drop some gifts off to you that you'll need in this cold world," Black Ice said while moving closer towards her.

Faith scooted back on the hospital bed, in fear, as he placed the items on the foot of the bed.

"Hmm," he grinned, showing off his pretty white teeth. "You're nowhere near ready," he smirked.

"Why would you say that?" Faith asked.

"You fear me. You shouldn't fear no man or woman, not even the devil. They should fear you and your anger," Black Ice responded as he turned towards the door.

Faith looked down at the foot of the bed and her face was filled with shock as she raised both of her eyebrows and stared at the items. He had placed a long flip knife with a wooden handle. The handle alone was from the tip of her fingers to her forearm and the blade was just as long. Next to it was a small, hand-held axe.

She mumbled, "So, you gave me weapons? What's stopping me from using them on you?"

Black Ice stopped in his tracks with his back still facing her, "For two reasons, first, you don't have the balls to attack me and secondly-"

Before he could finish his sentence, Faith had grabbed the long knife and small axe and leaped off the bed into the air smiling, knowing both weapons would split open his head. Black Ice tilted his head to the side and grinned. In one swift move, he did a spinning round house kick and his size thirteen boot slammed into her chest, knocking her back onto the bed, where she then bounced onto the floor, holding her chest.

"Uggh, ugh," she gasped for air trying to catch her breath.

"Secondly, baby girl, you don't have the skills yet. I have to train you before you can stand up to a real killer. I don't have any worries, though. You were born to be a serial killer. Hahaha!" Black Ice continued his statement and burst out with a wicked laugh.

"I'm nothing like you! I'm no serial killer!" Faith shouted, while feeling the rage grow deep inside of her.

The small axe ripped through the air at a rapid speed and Black Ice smoothly twisted his body to the side, as it flew right passed him just as the room door opened. Erika screamed in agonizing pain feeling the axe crack through the bones on the side of her face. She touched the axe with her hands, shaking nervously as her mind began to race. *'Pull it out, pull it out! No, no, I shouldn't. I should get a doctor,'* Erika thought to herself. Erika looked at Black Ice and Faith, turned around and took off running out of the room while screaming.

Black Ice began to smile wickedly. "So, are you going to sit your ass on the floor or finish her? Now, because of you, I have to kill everyone on this floor. We never leave witnesses or evidence around. Remember, always clean up your mess. Never leave body parts lying around. Hahaha!" Black Ice left the room, leaving his daughter behind.

"This can't be real. This can't be my life. Just when everything was going right, this shit happens. Antonio damn sure won't want me after this," Faith said to herself, but was interrupted by the screams coming from the hallway. Faith jumped off the floor and took out to the room door with the knife in her hand. When she entered the hallway, she couldn't believe her eyes. "What the fuck?"

She stood there feeling as if she just walked into a horror movie. Black Ice swung his machete and chopped off the arm of a Caucasian nurse. She watched her arm flip and flop on the floor like a fish out of water and her hand open and close, as if she was trying to grab something.

"Ahhh!" The chunky Caucasian nurse with the blonde hair hollered in excruciating pain, while stumbling to get away. She used her right arm to hold her shoulder, where her left arm should have been. Blood squirted out every time her heart beat. She leaned on the wall to keep from slipping on the blood, while trying to walk away from Black Ice. "Oh God, Oh God! Ahhhh, somebody help me! Help!" Black Ice smiled, ran up behind her and pushed the blade of his machete through her back, ripping through her chest and then, he pulled down. "Ughh!" The nurse screamed while gasping for air.

He pulled the machete out of her and she fell forward. Her body bucked on the ground, creating a huge puddle of blood. Black Ice walked over her now, dead body, down the hallway, and began whistling as he turned the corner.

A few feet away, he could see the nurse's station where three nurses were kneeled on the floor, trying to help Erika get the axe that was jammed in her face in a vertical angle.

Erika tilted her head up off the floor to get a better look pass the three women she worked with that was trying to help her. Her one eye focused and her heart raced as she seen the man in the brown, leather trench coat walking towards them, whistling the melody of 'Jesus Loves Me'. He stopped whistling as he got closer and began to just sing the words while twirling the machete.

"Yes, Jesus loves me. Yes, Jesus loves me. Yes, Jesus loves me because the bible tells me so."

Erika saw the bloody machete leave blood splatter on the walls as he continued to twirl it around in circles. "No, no!" she began to back pedal.

"Erika, you shouldn't move. Stay still," Barbara said. Barbara was older, maybe in her mid-thirties with brown skin, and a soft voice. She was bent over, trying to get closer to Erika to keep her from moving and hurting herself further.

Black Ice swung the machete with all of his might and the razor sharp blade went right through Barbara's face, sending the top half of her face up in the air. Black Ice never lost that wicked grin on his face as he watched part of her head float in the air.

"Hahahaha!"

Erika hollered as what was left of her friend's face landed on her lap and Barbara's eyes rolled around looking at her. Erika pushed the head off of her as Barbara's body hit the floor, causing a loud thump.

"Ahhhh!" The other two nurses screamed. Before the skinny one could turn around and get a good look at Black Ice, both of her arms were chopped off from the shoulders.

"Hahahaha!" he laughed again, watching her tiny body fall forward as she cried hysterically. The third nurse jumped up and ran into one of the rooms, shutting the door. "Real smart bitch, real fucking smart. Out of all places to run, you lock yourself in a room. Even if I didn't want to kill you, I have to now, for that stupid, typical ass move. You see this shit I have to deal with?" He looked back at Faith, who was still in shock watching him point his machete and turn to the room she just ran into. "You'd think these people never watched scary movies." He looked back behind him to see Erika pop up from the floor and take off running down the hallway towards the staircase. "We kill our own, babygirl. In other words, this mess is mine to clean, but her... you gotta get, Faith."

Faith looked at Black Ice as if he lost his mind, and then at Erika, stumbling down the hallway trying to get to the staircase.

"Damn, if she gets away and tells the police, I will never get away and live a normal life. I will never get to be with Antonio. No, this can't be my life. I can't be trapped in a life I don't control. I've lived that life once, I'd be damn if I live it again," Faith said out loud to herself, and then took off running passed Black Ice, jumping over the bodies and puddles of blood.

"That's my girl. Make daddy proud," he said, and then looked down at the floor to see the skinny woman with her arms chopped off, still alive using her legs to push her body, leaving smears of blood where both of her arms should have been. She was crying and trying her best to get away. "Now, ain't that a bitch. You know there used to be this popping dance back in my day called, The Worm. It sort of looks like what you doing, but you should flop your belly on the floor, too. You'll probably move a little faster, bitch. Damn, you brought back memories," he said and swung down hard with the machete, cutting off her right leg from the thigh.

"Ahhh! Lord help me! God, please help me! I have children. Don't kill me, don't kill me! My son and daughter need me. I'm all they have." The skinny woman begged and pleaded to Black Ice, while still trying to inch away.

"I'm tempted to leave you and see if you will survive. The fight you have for your life really intrigues me, bitch. Just look at you, literally, just fucking look at you. You're no more than a hundred pounds soaking wet, you have no arms and just one leg, and your ass is still trying to crawl away. I'm kinda shocked you didn't bleed to death. If I would have known you were this tough bitch, I would have made other plans for you. Only if I was a nice guy, but I'm not." He swung down again, chopping off the other leg. She screamed from the top of lungs for God to save her. "I don't think God can hear you," he told her and began to laugh as he swung down one last time, to cut her body in half. He began to whistle again as he continued his path back to the nurse that ran inside the patient's room.

Stephanie's body trembled. "Why did I leave my phone at the nurse's station?" she asked herself, while crying and breathing hard. The screams in the hallway finally stopped. "Go away, please just go away," Stephanie whispered, praying the psychopath in the hall would just leave, but she could still hear the deep tone singing Jesus Loves Me, which sent chills through her body. She heard the room door open and covered her mouth with her hand to keep from screaming.

"In all my years of killing, you have to be the dumbest bitch of them all." He reached around and grabbed her ankle from under the hospital bed.

"Ahhhh!" Stephanie screamed as loud as she could.

"You're really pissing me off. First, you run into a room that only has one way in and out, and then, you hide under the hospital bed, out of all places. I'm not going to even kill your stupid ass here. You don't deserve a fast death. I have worse plans for you," he informed as his foot came down on her face, knocking her out.

Black Ice began to drag her body out of the room, and then pulled out his phone to call his henchman that was waiting a few blocks away for his orders. "Kill the power, clean the mess up here and take as many women as you can, but don't touch Faith," Blake Ice ordered.

Faith's mind raced, thinking about all she will lose before even having it. She now stood in the hospital building staircase, looking over the rails and could see Erica, looking back up at her with one good eye and the axe stuck in her face. Jamaica Queens Hospital was a five story building but they were only on the third floor. Faith knew if Erika made it to the fourth floor lobby, it will be all over and there would be too many witnesses.

"I can't let this happen," she said out loud, just as it went completely black in the staircase.

Faith looked back behind her in the little glass window on the door she came from and it was completely dark through the whole building. She smiled an evil grin and quickly wiped it from her face as Black Ice's face popped up in her head, "I'm nothing like him, but this is perfect timing to get that fat bitch," she mumbled to herself and looked up at the emergency exit light.

"Ahhh!" Erika screamed, knowing she had to get away from Faith fast. The adrenaline in her body that was keeping her from feeling too much pain, was now running over as her body ached and her head began to throb and spin. "Got to keep moving, I can't die like this."

She could hear Faith's footsteps quickly catching up to her as she ran back down another flight of stairs. Erika sighed with hope as she could see the red exit sign, knowing she made it to the first floor lobby. She grabbed the doorknob of the steel door and Faith aimed and tossed the knife, slamming and ripping into Erika's hand and the steel door.

"Ahhh!" Erika hollered as she looked up and could see Faith a flight away, with a sick smile on her face. Erika's hand was now stuck in the door by the knife. She grabbed the long wooden handle with her left hand and pulled with all of her might, but the knife didn't budge. Erika turned around to see Faith walking down the stairs.

"No, no, not like this. I'm going to die an old lady, not like this!" She shouted while still pulling the handle, realizing she wasn't strong enough. She took a deep breath and pulled back the hand that the knife was stuck in, "Ahhhh!" she screamed as the knife ripped through her flesh, splitting her hand in half, "Ahhh!

Ughh!" Erika screamed, looking at her hand dangling like a piece of meat.

"Oh shit," Faith said, not knowing that Erika would go through the extreme of ripping her own hand in half to get away.

Faith stopped walking and started running towards Erika as she headed down the next flight of stairs. Faith grabbed the handle of the knife that was stuck in Erika's hand and in one swift pull, she yanked it out of the door. Erika made it to the basement floor and looked up to see a sign that read 'Parking Lot'. She reached for the door with her right hand and cried even more while looking down at it. For a brief second, she forgot she couldn't use it. She pulled her hand back and pressed it hard up against her breast to use as pressure to stop the blood and numb the pain. She used her left hand to open the door and run through.

"Ugh! Help! Help! Somebody help me!" she screamed as she stumbled through the parking lot, praying someone was coming to park their car or leaving out. She saw three men dressed in all black loading something into a white van through the emergency spot lights. "Help! Help!" she screamed, then stopped when she noticed they had masks on and were throwing patients into the van. She quickly scanned the basement and noticed five more vans of different colors with men loading more patients and nurses. "Ugh!" Erika groaned, while coughing up blood from feeling a sharp blade enter the center of her lower back. She then looked down and could see the knife poking from her stomach, dripping thick blood. She could now feel someone pressing against her back and lips pushing up on her ear.

"I bet at this moment, you wish your ass wouldn't have talked so much shit to me, huh bitch?" Faith taunted as she snatched the knife out and pushed it back into her back, and continued to stab her repeatedly.

"Please stop! Stop it, please," Erika cried as she fell to the floor and rolled over onto her back.

Faith stood there and stared at her, before she jumped on her and began to stab her in the chest and stomach. Blood splattered all over her as she heard Erika whimpering in a quiet, raspy tone, "Stop… please."

Faith couldn't if she wanted to at this point. She was beginning to have flashbacks of all the pain and beatings she took from her mother. All she could hear was her own voice as a child saying, *'Stop mommy. No, please stop.'*

Faith looked down at Erika with the axe still jammed into her face, damn near taking part of her face off and about nineteen stab wounds in the chest and stomach.

She stood up off of her, "What have I become? This isn't me. I'm sorry. I'm so sorry." Faith cried out as tears ran down her face.

"You're becoming who you were supposed to be, my child; a wolf, not a sheep, not a fucking victim." Faith heard a voice say in a very deep tone.

She turned around to see Black Ice holding a bloody machete in one hand and an ankle to an unconscious nurse in the other.

"This isn't right, it's wrong. We'll go to jail for this," Faith panicked while crying.

"Didn't I tell you that we're above the rules and everyone else follows? We are above the law! And my foolish child, there will be no trace in two minutes. My men cleaned the blood, took the security tapes, and cut the power. By the time the police notice something is wrong, they'll have no leads, just about fifteen women nurses and patients, missing without a trace. You checked in as Jane Doe, they have no name or record of you. Now finish that bitch off, so we can go," he ordered.

"Finish her off," Faith mumbled, wondering what he was talking about. She looked over to see Erika squirming around the parking lot, sliding in her own blood. "Oh shit, I almost forgot about her," Faith said to herself. "No, I won't finish her off. This isn't me. I'm not you!" Faith shouted.

"Listen, you little bitch. We don't have time for this back and forth shit. You are what the fuck you are, the child of the devil. Now, get your black ass over there and kill her! Now!" Black Ice shouted.

"No!" Faith screamed and threw her knife with every ounce of strength she had.

Black Ice stepped to the side and followed the knife with his eyes, as it slammed into the forehead of one of his henchmen that was loading the women into the van behind him.

"Isn't this how this all started in the first place, with you having a fuckin temper tantrum and throwing shit with no aim or practice?" he rhetorically asked as he watched his henchman fall to the ground dead, with blood leaking out of his head. He then turned around to face Faith, but to his surprise, she was gone. "Hmmm, maybe she has more of me in her blood than she knows."
He dropped the ankle of the nurse he was carrying and began whistling while walking up to Erika. Erika repeatedly coughed up blood and tried

to move, but couldn't. She looked up to see Black Ice standing over her.

"Children never listen and girls are worse with their emotional ass attitudes." That was the last thing Erika heard while watching Black Ice's foot stomp down on the axe that was jammed into her face. The axe went all the way through, cutting her face in half. The smell of feces hit the air as her bowels released seconds before she died.

Chapter 6

As soon as Faith threw her knife, she took off running for her life, back up the stairs to her room to grab the things that Dr. Monroe gave her. Once everything was cleared out, she headed to the street. It was 3a.m. and rain was pouring down as she walked the streets of Queens, NY in her hospital gown. Sirens could be heard coming at rapid speed, so she began to power walk down a backstreet behind Vanwyck Highway, to a block of private houses. She stopped in the middle of the block when she noticed a house boarded up. She opened the front gate that surrounded the house and walked around to the backyard. Faith pulled and removed the long wooden board that covered the back door and pushed the door open to enter the dark room.

She sat down on the floor and cried hysterically. "I'm not him or the hoe my mother wants me to be. This is my life. I choose who I am," she said to herself, over and over. She rocked back and forth while holding herself until she fell asleep.

Five hours later, sunlight peeped through the cracks of the wooden boards that covered the windows.

"Mmm," Faith moaned as the light hit her face. She opened her eyes and looked around, trying to figure out where she was. Then, it all came back to her, including everything that happened in the hospital.

She looked down at the dirty hospital gown that she still had on. She noticed that the rain rinsed off most of the blood, "Shit, what am I going to do? Where am I going to go?" she looked down in the hospital bag to see what Dr. Monroe had given her. Inside was a credit card, cellphone, and what appeared to be a keycard to a hotel, and a note telling her what to do.

Dr. Monroe pulled into his parking spot at his new condo. He walked into the lobby where the guy at the front desk nodded his head at him. Dr. Monroe removed his keycard from his pocket and swiped it across the scan to access the elevator. He got inside and pressed the button with number 17 on it and scanned his keycard once more, to enter the penthouse. He had on a grey suit that fit his body perfectly. As he walked into the penthouse, he removed his Glock 45 from the holster and cautiously walked inside. The first thing you can see, upon entering the penthouse, was an open kitchen with brown cabinets and marble countertops. As you step deeper into the penthouse, you'd reach the living room with all white furniture and a black throw rug. The view from the living room was remarkable; you could view the entire city through the large window that came from the floor to the top of the ceiling.

To the far left, you could see the master bedroom; one of the three rooms in the condo. Dr. Monroe let his gun lead the way as he could hear the shower running. He cautiously opened the door and the large canopy bed was the center of attention. He walked passed it onto to the master bathroom door. He scanned the room quickly and noticed about fifteen shopping bags of women's clothing and shoes. He opened the bathroom door and thick steam rushed towards him. He walked to the shower and could see a silhouette of a sexy woman with thick legs, and a body shaped like Serena Williams. He slid the glass door back and pointed the gun at the woman. She turned around and smiled, still washing her legs.

"So, you point your gun at everyone you give keys to your place?" Faith asked.

Antonio stood there, lusting over her, before her words sunk in his head, "No sweetie, I'm sorry," he replied while lowering the gun.

"Could you hand me a towel please?"

"Hmm, yes. Sorry," Taking his eyes off the perfect, chocolate woman, he reached over to hand her a towel.

Faith wrapped the towel around her and stepped out of the shower. "You have a beautiful place. I never seen anything like this in my life. And why do you have a gun?" Faith asked, while drying off, walking out of the bathroom.

Antonio walked into the master bedroom behind her, "I'm sorry for pointing the gun at you. To be honest, I wasn't really expecting you, but figured you were here because I get emails every time the credit card is used," he explained.

"Oh, so you want me to leave. I don't want to intrude," Faith said as her smile immediately left her face. She dug around in one of the bags to find the baby oil and rubbed it all over her body, without even making contact with Antonio. She reached and pulled out a purple thong and matching bra, then put them on.

"Wait, wait! I never said that. I want you here. I meant, I wasn't expecting you to be here, since the weirdness happened at the hospital. You didn't notice anything?"

"Notice what? I was supposed to leave today, but I couldn't stay any longer, so I left before I was even discharged," Faith said with a confused look on her face.

"Well, over seventeen people; staff and patients went missing last night. There was a black out at the hospital and almost everyone on the third floor just vanished in thin air. Traces of blood could be found, but the people don't know what the hell was been going on," he replied.

"So, that's why you carry a gun? And that's crazy, that so many people can just disappear," she said as flashbacks of Black Ice's henchmen loading people in the van, started playing in her head. *'I got to play it cool. I can't let him know what's going on. Maybe I can tell him the truth; that I have a super thug as a father I just met, that kidnaps people, kills them, and wants me to do the same thing. Yeah, I should tell him everything over lunch and everything will be okay. Yeah right. My past will be just that. This man is my future and present,'* Faith thought to herself then walked to him seductively. Antonio grabbed her into his arms and let his hands travel around her smooth, soft skin. The sight of her chocolate skin turned him on even more.

"You don't know how long I waited and wanted you in my arms, baby," he said in a deep sexy tone.

Their lips locked and they kissed passionately. Antonio removed his clothes while stepping forward, guiding her to the bed. He laid her down on the king size canopy bed and spread her legs. He moved her purple thong to the side and leaned in, taking her clit in his mouth. Faith moaned as her body tightened up. She removed her bra and began to play with her breast, rubbing her nipples.

'Damn, I'm surprised that I can still feel anything down there after what my mother did to me.' Faith thought, but her mind went blank as Antonio flicked his tongue up and down her clit, while gently sucking it.

"Mmm. Yes, shit!" she moaned while grabbing the back of his head.

"Mmm. You taste so fucking sweet," Antonio moaned while taking his middle finger and inserting it into his mouth, until it was nice and wet. Then, he slowly slides it into her tight pussy and worked it in and out, while sucking on her clit. He kissed and

99

sucked repeatedly, teasing her and pumped his finger faster while twisting and turning his finger with every pump. He came up for air and smiled, seeing her white cum cover his finger and running down his hand. He then slowly climbed on top of her and inserted the head of his dick in her, then worked the tip in and out, before pushing it all the way in.

His thick, seven-inch dick touched the back of her walls and he grinded slowly. "Ahh. Shhh. Oh yes, baby. Fuck me. Fuck me," she moaned, while wrapping her legs around his body.

"Fuck, fuck," he groaned, while looking at her with lust in his eyes. "In thirty-five years of my life, I never felt a pussy grip my dick like yours," he said out loud as he pulled out of her and went back down, taking her clit back into his mouth.

The sensation of his dick was still throbbing inside of her, even after he pulled out and his lips, now on her clit, drove her crazy.

"Oh God! Yes, baby, yes!" she screamed, while grabbing the sheets and she let go of her pounding orgasm. Her body went into convulsions as she climaxed multiple times, soaking the blue satin sheets.

"Damn, I never saw a woman cum so hard. You're so fucking sexy," he stated as his ego grew and his dick got even harder.

He flipped Faith around, arched her back and slid into her wet warm pussy. Faith could feel the veins on Antonio's dick throb inside of her. She slowly threw her ass back and Antonio watched his dick disappear into her sweet pussy and come back out. He thrust harder and could see her cum covering his thick dick, exciting him even more.

"Oh God, baby. You ain't going nowhere, baby. I'm never letting this good pussy go. Never," he groaned, while pounding her faster and harder, gripping her waist. He watched her ass shake, "Oh God, I can't take it!" he screamed as her pussy tightened around his dick. "Oh, God," he groaned and then pulled his dick out of her, jerking his dick sending white, thin cum over her ass cheeks.

"Mmm," Faith moaned and then turned around. She took his hard dick into her hands, slowly jerking him off, allowing her hands to travel up and down his shaft and around the tip.

"Sssh! Ohh! Fuck baby. It's so sensitive after I cum," Antonio said, while his body lightly trembled.

"Oh really," Faith replied and took the head of his dick into her mouth.

"Oh shit, baby. I can't take no more," he pleaded.

"Good," she replied, showing off her white teeth. She turned him around, forcing him to lay on his back, then climbed on top of him with her ass facing him. She inserted his rock hard dick into her pussy.

"Oh, baby. What you doing?"

"I'm going to fuck you until your dick can't take anymore," she said seductively. She closed her eyes and could feel his dick in her stomach. She rocked her hips back and forth, "Ssshhh fuck! Yes, baby," she moaned then started to bounce her body up and down. "Yes, yes, yes. Fuck, yes!" she screamed while bouncing herself harder on his dick.

Antonio looked on in amazement as she came what looked like a puddle of water. Her cum splashed onto his stomach and traveled down his dick and balls.

He smacked her ass. "I fucking love you!" he shouted.

Faith slowed down, but didn't stop bouncing, "Don't say it unless you mean it," she moaned as she turned around and looked at him.

"I mean it, baby, I mean it," Antonio said as she rocked herself harder back and forth on his dick, and he nutted all inside of her.

Chapter 7

For the next six months, life was like a dream for Faith. Living with Antonio was something in life that she had never experienced; so much joy, love, and having someone that truly cared for her. They had sex all the time and went out every once in a while, but that was okay with her. Faith was used to being trapped in the house for most of her life, so being trapped in a penthouse condo with everything she could ever want, was heaven to her. Everything was great, besides the fact that Antonio would go weeks without coming home.

'Damn, I miss him,' she thought. She sat naked on the white leather couch, which faced the windows to the view of the city. She sat quietly, thinking about everything with a cup of hot tea in one hand and her iPhone in the other hand.

I miss you. Can't wait until you come home baby.

She texted him and waited for a reply, but never got one. *'He's always working,'* She thought while sipping her tea.

She reached for her laptop that sat on the glass table in front of her. "Might as well shop."

Shopping online had become Faith's newfound all-time high. Antonio gave her a seven thousand dollar spending limit every month. She ordered some new lingerie from Victoria's Secret and a few new outfits.

"He would love these." Out of curiosity, Faith pulled up the Google search bar. "It's over, the past is the past. Why am I concerned about where I come from? None of that matters, look how I'm living." The curiosity drove her crazy. For the past few months, she was able to brush it off while Antonio was home, but now, she had nothing but time on her hands.

Her hands began to tremble, so she went on to type in Black Ice's name into the search bar and pressed enter. To her surprise, so many links pulled up on this name. She clicked the first link that read 'The Notorious

Serial Killer, Black Ice'. It took her to a main page and she began to read.

Real name, Michael Ice Sr., of Brooklyn, NY. Body count of murders are unknown. No evidence or traces of bodies have barely been found. Rumor has it, that he has pets, man-eating hyenas that dispose of the bodies. In the early 1980s-1990s, victims would appear missing body parts such as heads, hands, eyes, and even genitalia. There is another rumor stating that there is a trophy house in Brooklyn, where all the missing body parts could be found, but the home has never been located. Black Ice controls an organization with thousands of people that operates drug trades and kidnapping throughout the United States. Michael Ice Sr. was killed in 2014 by a special tactical army unit, alone with outside help...

Faith stopped reading. "Killed? That nigga far from dead. I'm a daughter of a fuckin psychopath killer," Faith said out loud.

"What psychopath killer, baby?"

Faith heard a voice behind her. She shut the laptop and turned around. "Nothing baby, just some mess I was reading online," she said as she got up from the couch and ran into his arms. "Oh my God baby, why didn't you tell me you were coming home? I would have tried to cook something for you."

"Now woman, you know damn well you can't cook. I'm not with you for that," he replied.

"Then, why are you with me?" she asked, while kissing him slowly.

"Well first, it's this chocolate skin complexion, so smooth, so soft, and such a turn on. Next, it's your hair. Then, it's your lips, so damn juicy and full." As Antonio spoke, he removed pieces of his three piece, tan colored suit. "It's your mind. How you are willing to submit to me and love me. Oh, and it's your sweet, that juicy sweet pussy," he said, while leading her to the large, open condo window. "I'm going to fuck you over the city," he whispered into her ear, while bending her over as she pressed her palms against the thick window.

He worked the tip of his dick in and out of her moist pussy until it fit all the way in. "Shhh.... mmm baby. I love you baby," she moaned as he thrust faster. She could feel his dick swelling up and veins throbbing. "Hold it, baby, don't cum yet! You better not cum, I'm almost there!" she screamed, while arching her back even more, so he could get deeper penetration.

"Ugghh!" Antonio groaned and pulled out, shooting cum all over her back.

"Smmh," Faith sucked her teeth. "Damn, I was almost there, but it won't be a problem. I can get you right back up," she said when she turned around and grabbed his now, soft dick.

"No sweetie, I'm good," he said, while back pedaling and pulling his dick out of her hands. He grabbed his boxer briefs and pulled them back up, along with his clothes.

"It's okay, we can start back up later. I need to shower anyway. You always cumming on my back. I miss you like hell though. So, where are we going to eat?" she asked as Antonio chuckled, with a fake laugh. "What did I say that was funny?" she asked, staring him down with a confused look on her face.

"Nothing baby. I just got to leave and get back to the hospital to work. Just order something," he replied.

"Wait, What? You just got here, Antonio. It's been nine days since I saw you and that's way too long to go without you. And plus, you work at night, it's 6:57a.m.!" she shouted.

"Listen, I shouldn't have to explain myself to you. I'm a grown ass man. You knew I was a doctor when we started this. I work a lot... that's nothing new. This big, beautiful condo that costs $800,000.00 that you're standing in right now. How you think I afford the mortgage for this place? How do you think I'm able to spoil your ass? It's because I work and I don't need you questioning that, baby. If I need to do a double shift and sleep at the hospital, so be it. You know I'll always come home. And when I do, I don't want or need the stress!" he shouted. He grabbed his blazer and headed for the elevator.

Faith looked at him weird for a second, and then ran over to him. "I'm sorry, I didn't mean to stress you, baby. I just want and need more time with you," she said, while tiptoeing to kiss the side of his neck. "I'm sorry I upset you."

He turned around to kiss her and their tongues danced in each other's mouth. Antonio broke their embrace. "It's okay, baby, I just need you to understand where I'm coming from. I'll see you soon." He kissed her on the forehead and entered the elevator.

Chapter 8

"Another week has gone by and I still haven't heard from him," Faith said out loud, while crying. She eventually cried herself to sleep on the couch.

A few hours later, she stretched, yawned, and looked around. "Damn, I must've overslept." She looked out the window. "The lights just seem so much brighter from up here." She got up and walked to the wall near the open kitchen and turned on the light switch. It made a clicking sound, but never came on. "Hmm, the light must have blown out. I'll have Antonio fix it or call maintenance tomorrow." Walking to the refrigerator to get something to drink, she noticed that the refrigerator light didn't come on either. "Come on!" Raising her left eyebrow, she said, "Power must be out in the whole building." Walking to the living room, she grabbed her cellphone to call Antonio, but the call didn't go through. "Stupid phone! Why the hell isn't there any signal in here?"

she asked out loud, and then heard the elevator open. "Baby, is that you?" she asked, squinting her eyes to focus on who came out of the elevator. The only light that entered the condo was from the building outside. She continued to look, but saw nothing. "Antonio, is that you?" she asked, thinking she heard large footsteps every once in a while, and then stop. She felt her stomach tighten up and her heart stop as she heard the familiar whistling melody of the song, Jesus Loves Me. "Oh shit!" she mumbled, knowing who it was, but she couldn't see.

"Do you think Jesus loves us?" she heard a voice whisper in her ear. Black Ice was standing right behind her.

"Ahh!" she screamed and stepped forward. She turned around, still trying to focus her eyes to the darkness. She could see his body frame, but not his face because he was that dark, but you could see his white teeth. "H-H How... how did you find me?" she stuttered and back pedaled away from him, hoping she could make it to the elevator to get away.

"Find you, child? I didn't have to find you; I already knew where you were. I've been patiently waiting on you to open your eyes," Black Ice told her in a deep tone.

"Open my eyes to what?" Faith asked.

"Open your fucking eyes and see this life isn't for you," Black Ice replied.

"Yes it is, this is what I want! I don't want to be like you. I'm not a fucking psychopath murderer like you. I'm happy and I'm in love, fuck you-"

Before she could finish her sentence, she felt a huge hand wrap around her neck and choke her. She then felt her self being lifted off her feet and them dangling back and forth.

"You know what," Black Ice said, while pulling her closer to his face, so that she could see his eyes, "maybe you're not like me, little bitch. Out of all my children, you're the slowest motherfucker I ever pushed out of these ball sacks. You didn't even sense me in this damn apartment. You don't know how to use the gifts you were born with! Hell, you ain't even using your common sense. You let everyone walk over you. Maybe you have more of your mother's blood in you... naw because even that bitch is more of a fighter than you. You like this stupid fantasy you live in when the reality is bullshit. What is it about this life you love? Is it the luxury, my child? Hmm?" Black Ice asked, while loosening his grip around her neck a little, just enough for her to get some air. She inhaled and exhaled three times, and then felt the grip tighten up again. "If it's luxury, my child, I'm richer than anyone you could ever meet. And rule number one: never depend on a nigga or his money, go get your own. What you earn, no man can take and no one can ever say what they gave you. So, is it luxury? Money? No, no, that's not it. You think you're in love, little bitch. Hahahaha! This is going to be fun. Love is an illusion, but this will be a perfect lesson for you. Love made me who I am once I realized it was nothing, but pain and love will make you who you are meant to be, my daughter. I will wait and watch. And if I see one more sign of weakness, I will end your life myself. But since you're so attached to this life, I dare you to follow your doctor friend once he leaves here. Hahaha!" Black Ice tossed her across the room. She felt herself go up in the air then hit the marble floor hard.

"Ughh!" she screamed out in pain.

"You're either a sheep or a wolf, my child. You can't be both." And with those words spoken, Black Ice disappeared into the darkness again.

She opened her eyes and the lights came back on. She quickly ran to the kitchen and grabbed the biggest knife and searched the entire condo, but there was no sign of Black Ice. She scratched her head, trying to figure out how he got in and out of the condo when the elevator is the only way in. She sat down on the couch and felt something hard beneath her. She got up to see what it was and stood there frozen. The small axe that was stuck in Erika's face was now cleaned and placed right next to the flip knife with the wooden handle. On top of her weapons was a note that read: *'Sheep or wolf?'*

Chapter 9

Faith stayed up all night doing more research on Black Ice, while his words kept replaying in her head. *'Out of all my children, you are the slowest one.'*

"That means I have siblings and are they like me? Is this feeling I get an urge for me to kill or the enjoyment of feeling others in pain? Or is it the more upset I get, the less pain I feel and the better my mind works? And what the hell did he mean by this is a fantasy? This is the life I want to live. I'm happy and Antonio loves me."

She closed the laptop and got off of the bed, feeling stupid that she let Black Ice's words get to her. She got undressed and went into the bathroom to run a bubble bath, and then stepped into the tub full of hot, bubbled water.

"Oh Lord, yes. This is so refreshing," she said as she pushed the button to turn on the tub jets then started to whistle a familiar melody... Jesus Loves Me. It took her about five minutes of her whistling the melody before she realized what she was doing. "Why did I just do that shit? The song must've been stuck in my head, that's all."

"What song?" Antonio said as he walked in the bathroom.

She looked up to see him, "Nothing baby. I'm excited to see you here, being without you is unbearable at times."

He looked down at her and got undressed. "I'm here now, my love." He got completely naked and stepped in the jetted tub bubbled water with her.

"How was your day, baby? Did you eat? I miss your cooking."

"Shhh, stop talking and come here," he said seductively.

Faith stood up and lowered herself on top of him, sliding his thick dick inside of her warm pussy. She rocked back and forth while staring into his eyes. Antonio leaned back and grabbed her small waistline.

"Ohh baby, why does this pussy feel so sweet?" he groaned as his facial expression twisted up in pleasure.

"Oh hell no baby, don't cum, you better not cum! Don't you cum," she moaned and started rocking her hips even slower in hopes of keeping him from cumming before she got to really enjoy feeling him inside of her. "I love you. I really love you. You are the best thing that ever happened to me," she moaned, while starring at him with bubbles splashing everywhere.

"I love you, too baby. Now, fuck me faster," he groaned, while grabbing her waist even tighter, forcing her hips to grind faster.

"No baby. Ssshh. No, I don't want to rush," she said in between her moans, but her words were going into deaf ears.

"I love you. I fucking love you!" he shouted and released inside of her.

Faith rolled her eyes and sucked her teeth. "You've been doing that a lot lately and it's not fair. I be right there, ready to cum. You should let me get mines," she demanded and could feel his dick go soft inside of her, to the point she no longer felt it. She eased off of him and sat back in the warm water. Antonio stood up, kissed her on the forehead, and then walked over to the shower and hopped in. Ten seconds later, he stepped out, drying off his body. Faith still sat in the tub watching him with lust in her eyes.

"Damn, I couldn't ask for a better man or life." He began to put back on his suit and her lust turned into anger because she knew he didn't like wearing clothes in the house. "Wait, where are you going? Why are you getting dressed?" she questioned, now standing up in the bathtub. "Please tell me you're not about to leave so soon when you just got here. I haven't spent real time with you in weeks."

"We went through this yesterday. I told you I work a lot. I have no time to lay around and play house, so don't stress me out about it. We just had a good time. Go shop online or you can leave the house. I like keeping you to myself, but some fresh air would do you some good," he said as he finished getting dressed and headed for the elevator.

'Follow him!' Faith could hear Black Ice's voice loud and clear in her head. She dried off and threw on a purple sweat suit that had a hoodie on it that hugged her body like a glove. She grabbed some money off the top of the dresser, her cellphone, and ran for the elevator.

"Come on, come on," she said, while pushing the button. A smile spread across her face when the elevator arrived. She rode it down to the lobby. "I hope you haven't left already." She stepped outside just as the green Mercedes S550 was pulling out of the private parking lot. Faith could see him talking on the phone, waiting for traffic to slow down, so he could pull off and merge into traffic. "Yes," she said as a yellow cab pulled up to the building and a lady hopped out. Faith quickly jumped in.

"Where to miss?" the Indian cab driver asked her in his thick accent.

She turned around and seen Antonio pull out of the parking lot to the street. "Here is two-hundred dollars. I need you to follow that green Mercedes Benz and there will be more money in it for you, just don't lose him."

The cab driver smiled and took the money. "Yes miss, I know the routine. I have done this plenty of times. A wife always wants me to follow their husband. I will ask no questions as long as the pay is good," he said and pulled off, staying one car behind Antonio's Mercedes Benz to keep from being noticed.

'I always wonder what the outcome be to the women that follows their husbands,' Faith thought to herself, afraid to say it out loud to hear his answers. She relaxed when she noticed they were driving down Jamaica Avenue coming close to the hospital where he worked. She felt relief.

'I don't know why I even listened to that man who supposed to be my so called father. Black Ice just put doubt and worries in my head for

nothing. I have the perfect life now and the perfect man that truly loves me. Black Ice is trying to force that this life isn't for me,' she thought to herself and raised her hand to tell the cab driver to turn around and take her home, but she stopped when she noticed they zoomed passed the hospital.

"What the fuck? That nigga said he was going back to work. Let me not jump to conclusions, maybe he's about to get something to eat," she told herself, but her stomach told her that wasn't the case.

They drove down the road for about an hour and then, they reached a bridge that said 'Welcome to Long Island New Hyde Park'. They drove ten blocks then turned left. Faith's eyes widened as the homes got bigger and bigger.

"I've never seen houses this big," she said out loud.

"Yes, these homes are really big. Out of my price range. Mostly doctors, lawyers, and entrepreneurs live in this area."

They watched the green Mercedes Benz pull up to a large, two story brick mansion. The cab driver pulled up across the street as they noticed one of the doors of the three car garage lift up and Antonio pulled in.

"Wait, this isn't right. He never told me about this place," she said out loud to herself.

"That's what most women say when they have me follow their husbands. They never knew about the second house or apartment. If you want my advice, Miss, if you are happy, don't go looking deeper for problems. Go back home or you'll find what you've been looking for," the cab driver told her in his thick Indian accent.

"No, no. Maybe it's his friend's house or a family member. He wouldn't lie to me, he loves me." Faith passed the cab driver another hundred-dollar bill. "Wait here, I'm going to get a closer look," she said as she stepped out of the cab to cross the street.

"I warned you, Miss, the outcome is never good." She heard him say and she turned around, noticing he pulled off.

"Wait, Wait!" She shouted and waved her hands in hopes he would stop, but he disappeared down the block. "Great, there's my fucking ride. I'll just call another cab. Besides, he didn't know what he was talking about. I'll find what I'm searching for and that's me looking like a fool for coming here and letting Black Ice get to me," she said as she walked up the driveway.

She reached the chestnut double door and raised her hand to knock. "What the hell am I doing?" she asked herself and lowered her hand and turned to walk away.

"Baby, I need you to get ready for our date tonight. I've been dying to see this play on Broadway!" a voice shouted that was familiar to Faith.

Faith froze in her tracks when she heard Antonio shouting in the house. "What the fuck?" she said to herself and snuck around to the side of the house. She made her way in the backyard, where she could see a pool and behind it was a small basketball court. She walked closer to the house and could see a double glass sliding door. She walked up to the sliding glass door and slid it open. "Rich people, you'd think they'd lock their doors since they have so much to lose or maybe these stupid motherfuckers don't think they can be robbed because they stay in this boogie neighborhood."

She cautiously stepped in the house and there she was, standing in a huge kitchen. She tiptoed, walking deeper into the home, following the voices. She could see the living room where a beautiful light skinned woman stood in a black dress that hugged her body, even though she was slim. Faith could see she had a nice butt and from the look of her hands and neck, she could tell the woman was in her mid-thirties. But by looking at her body, there was no way you could tell her real age. She had on a diamond tennis bracelet with a necklace to match.

Two teenage boys walked up to the lady, "Mom, don't forget, we're spending the night at Maeko's house tonight," one boy said.

"You know I hate y'all over there. What kind of mother names their child Maeko? I know; a rapper groupie, Internet slut. Out of all the young men, why can't any of your friends have better futures like becoming lawyers, engineers, or doctor like your father? What do I always say?" The woman asked, while looking at the boys that were taller than her.

Faith couldn't believe they were calling her mom since they were so big and tall.

"You say the connections we make today will be the connection we will use tomorrow," the boys said simultaneously.

Faith continued to walk with a confused look on her face. Then she heard something that sounded like tap dancing on the hardwood living room floor. Her eyes followed the noise to see a little brown Pomeranian dog that jumped up into the woman's arms and she cuddled it like a baby.

"Dear, I'm almost ready. I had to feed Veronica," Antonio said, coming down the stairs and then into the huge living room, holding a two-year-old little girl that looked just like the woman. He walked to the beautiful woman in the black dress and leaned down to kiss her on the lips.

For the first time, Faith got to see the two boy' faces and they were identical twins, looking just like a younger version of Antonio with no facial hair.

"Ahhh! What the fuck! What the fuck?" Faith shouted. The sound of her voice caused everyone, including the dog, to look in her direction.

"Call the cops!" the woman said loudly over the dog barking.

"No! Don't!" Antonio yelled.

"You motherfucker! I thought you said you loved me, that you cared for me, that I was wifey. Seven months, Antonio! Seven months and you have a whole got damn family!

How could you do this to me? How could you do this to us?" Faith shouted.

"Oh, that's why you don't want us to call the police because this is one of your hoes, Antonio?" the woman shouted.

"Sabrina, baby, I'm sorry. Let me explain, baby. It was a mistake," Antonio said in a shaky voice and started walking towards Sabrina, trying to kiss her, but she pushed him away.

"It was a mistake? A fucking mistake? This is the third woman this year! Shit, this year ain't even over yet. Did you use a condom with this one? The last one we had to give fifty-thousand just to get her to have an abortion!" Sabrina shouted over the barking dog.

"No baby, I put Plan B pills in her drinks and water. She's a nobody," he replied to his wife, fearing what she may do.

"A nobody? A nobody? How the fuck can you say that?" Faith ran up on him and punched him in the jaw while he was still holding his daughter. The twin boys quickly grabbed Faith and pinned her down.

"Calm down before you make a mistake and hit my fucking sister!" One of the boys shouted, but his words did little to calm her down.

"Why? Why would you fucking do this to me? I love you…"

"Shut up! Just shut the fuck up!" Antonio shouted as his daughter cried in his arms. "I never loved you, you stupid bitch. I'm a sex addict. I'm addicted to it and can't control myself. You were young, dumb, and naïve to believe everything I said. I'd come fuck on my lunch break or just come for an hour and leave. You have no family, well, no one that cares about you. You needed me and a place to stay, so I used you, bitch. I will never leave my family for you or no bitch. I love my children. My twins are going to be pro-athletes and play basketball, and my wife is perfect in every way. I just need new pussy on the side every now and then. In this case, it happened to be yours. I don't love you, nor do I want you."

Faith stopped squirming around as the boys held her down on the floor. Her body trembled. It felt as if he used his words to pull her heart and chop it into little pieces. She laid there frozen.

"A place to stay?" Sabrina looked back at her husband, "This same place must be the condo you kept telling me was being remodeled. This is why you were keeping me away from it because you had some hoe in our shit?"

"Baby, exactly, some hoe. I felt sorry for the bitch because she had nothing and no one. That was it. I was never really there with this bitch. She means nothing to me," he told her.

Faith just looked at him with pain in her eyes, not believing what he was saying about her.

"Aww. Damn, it looks like you broke the little bitch's heart. I told you to quit fucking these strays. Peasant ass bitches. We always have to end up paying these bitches off. Sweetie, how much is it going to cost to pay your ass off? Name your price," Sabrina asked in a condescending tone, while bending down, looking at Faith.

Tears streamed down the side of Faith's face. It took her a minute to register what Sabrina had asked her. Her whole body ached with a pain that she had never endured.

"My price? Bitch, what the fuck you mean, *my price*?" Faith snapped. She couldn't believe this woman just asked her that. "Ughh! Ahhh!" Faith hollered and bucked her body, knocking both twins off of her. The twin boys fell to the ground.

"Who the fuck? Where did all that strength come from?" one of the boys asked in concern.

Before they could get up, Faith did a spin kick to Sabrina's stomach, sending her and the brown Pomeranian that was still in her arms, flying backwards.

"You bastard! I swear I will make you pay!" Faith shouted and sent a right jab into Antonio's left eye.

"Ahh! Ughh!" he groaned in pain and stumbled backwards.

Faith grabbed his two-year old daughter's hair and yanked the child out of his hands, and on to the ground.

"Ahhhh!" Baby Veronica laid on the floor, crying from the pain of bumping her head and fear running through her body.

"This is what you love? This is what you chose over me? Our relationship was a game, huh? I'll show you a motherfucking game. I promise you that!" Faith shouted and raised her leg, pulling it back and kicking baby Veronica in the stomach with all her might. She raised her hands in the air with a smile on her face and screamed, "GOAL!" as Veronica slid across the floor a few feet and under the glass coffee table. Antonio, Sabrina, and the twin boys, Calvin and Carlton, looked at her in horror. "I'll show y'all motherfuckers a game. You messed with the wrong one!"

"Ahhh! Ahahaa!" Sabrina screamed at the sight of her daughter balled up in fetal position, crying hysterically.

Faith wasted no time attacking Antonio. "I'll kill you! You hurt me like no other! My father was right!" she shouted and kicked Antonio in the balls.

"Ugghh!" he gasped for air as he choked on his own saliva.

She bent down close to his face, "I trusted you. I loved you with all my heart. You hurt me more than my mother ever had," Faith said through her clenched teeth.

The twins looked at her and knew they couldn't take this crazy woman head on. One of them ran in the kitchen to grab the small fire extinguisher and ran next to his brother. They smiled simultaneously, knowing exactly what each other was thinking. Calvin walked softly behind Faith and swung the fire extinguisher, slamming it into the back of her head and sent her crashing to the floor. The twins then jumped on her, punching and kicking her repeatedly, and then hit her in the head once more with the fire extinguisher.

"Stop, stop!" Antonio shouted after finally catching his breath. He walked up to Faith's body to touch her neck. He felt a pulse. "Thank God, she's still alive, but she's losing a lot of blood," he stated, while looking at the blood pouring from the back of her head.

"Thank God she's still alive? This bitch deserves to die! I'm calling the police and getting your little slut locked the fuck up! She kicked my baby and I don't see you over here checking on her, but you're over there checking on some hoe you were fucking that caused pure chaos in our home!" Sabrina shouted, while holding her daughter.

"No, it's not like that. Our sons don't need a fucking murder charge on their records," Antonio reasoned with Sabrina as he walked over to her and checked Veronica's ribs to see if they were broken. "She's fine."

"She should have been the one you checked on first instead of your hoe!" Sabrina shouted with an attitude and grabbed the iPhone out of her purse.

"No, baby, don't call the police," Antonio begged.

"Give me one reason why the fuck not. Now, you're trying to protect your slut?" Sabrina screamed.

"No, you stupid bitch! Our sons beat her inches from death. That shit will follow them for the rest of their lives and we can forget about getting them into a great college with that on their records. So, there goes another one of your meal tickets. Next, I can lose my license over some shit like this, so there goes this comfortable lifestyle we love and worked so hard for. We lose everything over a slut," Antonio replied.

"So what should we do then? I blame you for this shit!" she responded.

"We clean out the condo and drop this bitch off in the middle of nowhere. If she bleeds to death, so be it. If she doesn't, it'll be her word against ours and who is going to believe a worthless bitch? So, here is the plan, the boys will drop her off in the middle of nowhere, we go to the play as planned, and the boys go to their friend's house. We all have witnesses and an alibi for where we were," Antonio explained.

"But what if the little bitch comes back? She's crazy. You saw what she just did," Sabrina said worried.

"Easy, we kill her for breaking in next time. I keep enough firearms in the house and I really doubt she will be back. The thought of me not wanting her, broke her. Hell, she might even kill herself," Antonio answered confidently.

The twins quickly grabbed some rope and tied Faith's unconscious body and carried her to the black Cadillac Escalade truck, while Antonio and Sabrina cleaned the blood and all evidence that she was even there.

"This better work. I swear, if another one of your bitches pop up and cause more issues to our family, I'm divorcing your ass and finding another doctor that can keep his dick in his pants," Sabrina said meaning every word.

"You'll never leave me. I won't let you. I promise, she is the last one.

I'll clean out the condo tomorrow and we'll start all over," Antonio said, while pulling her closer and kissing her deeply.

"Yea, yea, it won't be that easy to get out of the doghouse," Sabrina replied.

Chapter 10

Carlton drove down the street following the speed limit; something he barely does. His brother, Calvin, sat in the back with Faith's body tied up on the floor.

"Yo, she's still bleeding. We gone have to clean the truck when we drop her off," Calvin said.

"Why should we drop her off so fast, after she hurt our sister? Why should she get off so easily?" Carlton asked, while stopping at the red light.

"What do you mean and what are you trying to do?" Calvin asked.

"I say we pick up Maeko and Travis and have some fun with her. Let's take her back to the condo before we drop her off. Did you see that bitch's body? She's short, thick with a fat ass. Why should dad be the only one to have a little fun with her?" Carlton looked back at his brother, waiting for him to agree.

"I agree," Calvin said as he bent over to squeeze her left ass cheek.

They pulled up to a large three story house and a dark skinned boy came out, followed by his Latino cousin the same age as the twins, which they were all sixteen years old. Maeko and Travis have been best friends with the twins since the third grade.

"So, we're really going to do this shit?" Maeko asked.

"Yea, why not? She means nothing to the world," Carlton answered.

As they pulled into the underground parking lot to the condo, they carried Faith to the private elevator and rode it to the penthouse.

"How can you hurt? How can you lie to me?" Faith whispered. Her head throbbed, but she could feel someone on top of her and inside of her. She tried to move but couldn't, so she opened her eyes to see a younger version of Antonio on top of her, bumping in and out of her pussy. She began to panic trying to figure what the hell was going on. She wiggled and squirmed until she realized that she was tied down with a

140

thin piece of rope that wrapped around her shoulders to her waist, making it impossible for her to use her arms. She was naked with her legs busted wide open for the young men to have their way with her.

"I told you this bitch had good pussy, B. I can see why dad was fucking her," Carlton said as he pulled out of her and pulled the condom off.

Calvin entered the room and flipped Faith over and arched her ass in the air. He put on a condom, eased inside of her and began to pound away.

'How?' Faith thought to herself as tears streamed down her face. She was now in the same position she fought her whole life to escape; a man forcing himself inside of her that she didn't love nor care for. Her body was numb to what the young men were doing to her. Her mind was gone and her heart was broken into pieces.

"Yo, this bitch pussy hella good, but she doesn't moan. That's such a turn off. All this wet, good pussy and she's not even screaming. I know I got a big dick," Calvin said and pulled out of her.

"I bet I can make this bitch scream," Maeko wagered.

Faith could feel her body being picked up and carried to the bathroom. He bent her over the bathtub and spit on his hand to moisten the tip of his dick and forced it into her ass.

"Ahhh! Ahhh!" Faith let a scream for the first time.

"Yeah, I knew I could get you to scream, bitch," Maeko said, while thrusting in and out of her.

Calvin, Carlton, and Travis came to the bathroom doorway with their shirts off, watching. "I don't even know why they got you tied up. I want you squirming and wiggling around more," he said as he loosened the ropes that kept her tied up.

"No, Maeko don't do that. She's dangerous," Calvin shouted just as Maeko slammed the door closed in his face and locked the door. Calvin shook his head in disbelief and the three teenagers went into the living

room and sat on the couch, and turned
on the TV.

Chapter 11

"Man, Maeko buggin by untying that bitch. I can feel it," Calvin stated.

"She's a damn woman that's half the size of all of us," Travis said, while rolling up the blunt and lighting it.

"That ain't no normal bitch. She kicked my sister across the room and screamed goal as if she was playing soccer. And the bitch had the nerve to be smiling the whole damn time. Then, she fucked up my dad in two moves. Had that nigga choking on his own spit," Carlton explained.

"She kicked your sister across the room? Ain't your sister like two years old or something? Hahaha," Travis laughed out of control, while smoking his weed.

"Shut up, that shit ain't funny. Pass the damn blunt," Carlton said and snatched the blunt out of Travis' hand.

"My bad, my bad," Travis said, while trying to control his laughter, "It's the weed, fam, but there's four of us. If she acts up, we'll beat that bitch ass and kick her across the floor," Travis replied.

Maeko had now lifted Faith up off the bathtub and leaned her over the sink, "These niggas acting all scared of you, but I'm not bitch. It should be me you fear with that good pussy and ass. How the fuck can a nigga use a condom? You going to enjoy this." He pulled her hair and worked his way into her sore anus.

Faith's tears slowed down as her anger raised. Her face tightened up and her mind went blank for a second. *'You're a wolf or a sheep?'* Black Ice's words echoed in her head over the moaning and groaning Maeko was doing, as if he was a porn star.

"I'm a wolf!" she screamed and grabbed her toothbrush out of the cup holder on the counter. "You motherfucker!" she screamed, while twisting around with his dick still inside of her and jammed the toothbrush into his left eye. His eyeball popped like a grape squeezing between someone's fingers.

Puss mixed with red blood oozed out of his eye socket, "Ahhhh! I'll fucking kill-" Before Maeko could finish screaming in pain, Faith grabbed the curling iron and jammed it down his throat. "Ughh, Ugh," Maeko choked and gagged for air.

"What's wrong, baby? You can't deep throat? You can't take nothing forced down that tight hole of yours?" Faith taunted sarcastically, and then smiled as she shoved the curling iron further back, sending it deeper down his throat.

Maeko bent over in excruciating pain, unable to breathe and see clearly.

"Here, let me show you how to deep throat, you little bitch," Faith said and got down on her knees.

She laughed when she saw that his dick was still hard. She took his dick into her hand and Maeko tried to push her away, but didn't have the strength from the lack of oxygen. He tried to focus all of his attention on removing the curling iron from his throat, but his muscles had swollen around it making it harder to pull it out, so he tried concentrating on breathing through his nostrils.

"First, you got to wet your mouth. If you try to deep throat with a dry mouth and throat, it will hurt like hell and that long pipe can fuck up your throat, making it sore," Faith said, and then took his six-inch dick into her mouth. She pushed it all the way to the back of her throat, and locked down with her teeth on his dick like a Pit Bull and shook her head side to side.

"Ugghhhh!" Maeko tried to scream, but couldn't get it out. He swung, punching her in the side of the face with the little strength he had left, but it did little to get her off of him. If anything, it made her sink her teeth deeper in his dick.

The taste of blood dripped down the back of her throat like warm tomato soup. She knew she was getting closer to her goal, so she shook her head even harder and yanked away, ripping off his dick.

"Ugghh! Ughhhh!" Maeko screamed the best he could.

Faith stood up, tilted her head back and used her hand to pull his dick from her throat. "See, you fucked up. Your first mistake was raping me in my own house and the second mistake was untying me. Y'all little niggas aren't very intelligent." Maeko grabbed his groin area as blood gushed out all over the bathroom floor. He slipped backwards and his back hit the tub. "The good news is you're going to bleed to death. The bad news is it won't be soon enough before I'm done with you," she said with a Kool-Aid smile on her face.

She turned to the sink and bent over into the cabinet. She grabbed a pair of razor sharp scissors and a twelve-inch black dildo. Maeko's eyes opened wide. She bent down and moved his hand from his groin area. He tried his best to keep his eyes open, but the loss of blood drained him. She stared, admiring her work, as she grabbed his nut sack and cut it off with the scissors. He squirmed and screamed the best he could, but it was all muffled.

"I'll keep these to remember you by," she said, then stood up and placed them into the cup she kept her toothbrush in.

"Ugghh!" Maeko tried to cry out when she lifted him up and bent him over.

She spit on the head of the dildo and tried to spread his ass cheeks, but Maeko clenched them extremely tight.

"No, no, no," he mumbled and wiggled around with the little energy he had left.

"Aww, you're trying to keep it tight," Faith said, and then smacked his ass and leaned over his back. "Remember when you said you're the one I should fear? Well, you were wrong, little bitch, it's me you should have feared. Before you die, know that you're going to hell with no dick, no balls, and a dildo stuck up your ass. Ahahaha!" Faith busted out laughing, and then rammed the dildo up his tightened ass. Maeko somehow gagged up the curling iron and screamed with all of his might before he died.

"Yo, what the fuck was that? Sound like Maeko screaming," Carlton said and sat up on the couch in attention.

"I thought I was hearing things since I'm high, but he has been in there a while with that hoe. I'm ready to slide in her again. It's time to switch," Travis said.

"Man, listen, we're all high as fuck, but I can feel something isn't right," Carlton said as the three of them got up and walked to the master bathroom.

Calvin knocked on the door three times, "Yo, Maeko, you aight, B?" Calvin shouted, but got no answer. "He's not answering," Calvin said.

"I'm telling you, something isn't right. Travis, break down the door, man," Carlton said as his heart raced and flashbacks of Faith's smile played in his mind, as she kicked his dad in the balls.

"This isn't right; we should just leave. Everything in my stomach is telling me to run," Calvin said while looking at his twin brother.

"Yeah, you're right," Carlton replied.

"Fuck that! Y'all trippin, my cousin in there and you two are talking about running. We're not going anywhere. Plus, we got to drop this bitch off and clean this place up before your father comes to check on it tomorrow. Now, stop acting like punks and help me break this fucking door down!" Travis shouted.

Faith could hear them arguing outside the door and the sound of weight slamming on the door followed. A wicked smile spread across her face as she grabbed a bobby pin off of the sink counter and a washcloth. She held the bobby pin with the washcloth, making sure it didn't touch her skin, and then she jammed it into the electrical socket on the wall. Sparks went flying and the lights in the condo flickered until everything went pitch black.

"Oh shit, what was that?" Travis shouted, realizing he couldn't see his hand in front of his face.

Carlton, Calvin, and Travis pulled their phones out of their pockets to use them as flashlights.

The bathroom door cracked open with an eerie sound. "Who did that? Did you open the door, Travis?" Carlton asked.

"Hell no, that wasn't me," Travis replied.

"Man listen, this is how horror movies start before everyone dies. I'm sorry, but I'm getting out of here. I'm listening to my gut feeling," Calvin said and turned around to walk out of the master bedroom.

"You right, bro, but if the power is out, the elevator won't work and it's the only way in and out of here," Carlton mentioned.

"Nah man, there's some type of emergency power on that shit or something. This is a high scale building. They can't keep these rich folk stuck up in here in the dark," Calvin told him.

"Alright, I'm coming with you. I have the same feeling," Carlton said and walked towards his brother.

"Fuck both of y'all. Y'all just gone leave me here to check on my cousin by myself and run around in the dark, of which happens to be YOUR father's condo! I see how y'all get down," Travis said with an attitude.

"Yo, I know you feel something isn't right and I'm not sticking around to find out. I'll leave it to my dad to fix this issue with his crazy bitch in the morning. We're out," Calvin stated.

"Fuck you both!" Travis shouted and felt something brush against his arm. He turned around with his phone to see what it was, but saw nothing. He slowly scanned the room with light from his phone. "Damn, these niggas got me buggin. Fuck outta here, making me feel like I'm feeling shit on me. Next, I'll be seeing shit," Travis said in a deep Spanish accent, and then turned back around to the bathroom. "Fuckin pussies," he mumbled to himself, while letting the light from the phone lead the way.

He stepped deeper into the bathroom and felt something wet and sticky on the floor. He looked down to see his white Jordan sneaker was now covered in blood. "What the fuck?" He followed the trail of blood to the bathtub and he squinted his eyes, trying to figure out what he was looking at. He then realized that it was his cousin bent over the bathtub with something stuck up his ass, just dangling between his butt cheeks. Travis focused his eyes to see the black object had veins and was shaped like a thick dick. "Oh shit, that's a dildo! What kind of freaky shit y'all got going on in here, Maeko?"

Travis didn't get a response.

"Maeko, you okay man?" he asked.

He moved closer and turned over his cousin's body. Travis' eyes grew wide at the sight of his naked body with blood pouring from his mouth and groin area, where his dick and balls should have been.

"Maeko! Maeko! Oh shit, oh shit!" Travis screamed, and then heard a noise behind him.

He turned around, looked up and down, but all he saw was darkness. He heard another sound and turned back around to see his cousin's body had been flipped back over on its stomach. He scanned his body to see the dildo that was once there, was now gone. He looked around the bathroom, still using his phone for light but couldn't find it. He heard, yet again, another noise behind him, but this time, he swung hitting nothing.

"I'm going fucking crazy. You guys, I think that bitch killed Maeko," he said with tears in his eyes. "And I think she raped him with a rubber dick!" he shouted, but got no response.

He raised his phone and saw Faith standing right in front of him, with blood dripping from the side of her mouth with a psychopathic smile on her face. "Ahhhh!" he screamed out of shock and swung his fist, aiming for the side of her face.

Faith ducked and dodged his blow, and then rose up while he was still screaming and pushed the long, black dildo down his throat.

"Ughhh!" Travis gasped for air. The smell hit his nose and he could taste shit in the back of his throat. His eyes watered up even more as he remembered the dildo was just in his cousin's ass. Travis was taller and stronger than Maeko. He grabbed the end of the dildo and pulled it out while gagging.

Faith smiled once the light went out and sneaked out of the bathroom. Her dark skin tone made it impossible to see her, blending in perfectly in the dark condo. She crept into the living room and grabbed the small axe and flip knife from under the couch that her dad left for her.

Travis had one more inch of the dildo to pull out, *'Oh, I'm going to beat this little bitch ass as soon as I'm able to breathe right,'* he thought, while bending over with his hands on his knees to catch his breath.

Faith raised the axe and swung hard. The blade ripped into the thick meat on the right side of his neck, "Ahhhh!" Travis screamed and stumbled backwards. Faith yanked the axe out of his neck and swung again. This time, Travis raised his arm and blocked the blow. The axe ripped through his forearm, tearing through his flesh. The sound of his bones cracking could be hard echoing through the bathroom. "Ahhh!" he screamed.

Faith swung twice, watching his arm hit the floor. She looked down at his arm twitching on the floor, and then stared at her axe. "Hmmm, I need to sharpen this. It should have cut through you much faster."

Blood squirted from where Travis' arm used to be and gushed out of the open wound in his neck. He pedaled backwards until he tripped over Maeko's body. He raised his other arm when he saw Faith about to swing the axe again, but she stopped before she swung. She looked into his eyes while he was begging for his life.

"Aww, you poor baby. You want me to stop?" Faith asked in a sarcastic tone. "But did y'all motherfuckers stop when you took turns raping me? My eyes begged for you to stop, the back of my head ached, and this bitch ass of a man tore my life apart! But, that wasn't enough pain for me, huh? You young fucks needed to see fit and rape me, so I don't feel sorry for your pleading or your crocodile tears." She then swung again and chopped off his left arm. "Much better, went straight though that time. Maybe because I added a little more power to that one." Then she cut deeper into the side of his neck. He screamed and yelled in pain, praying for her to stop, but his prayers went on to death ears. The daughter of the devil was the only one listening. She chopped three more times and looked overjoyed at her work.

Faith walked over to the sink and went back into the cabinet. "Perfect," she said and grabbed the pink bottle of Nair.

"Did you hear that?" Calvin said, while pressing the elevator button repeatedly.

"Yea, it sounds like Travis screaming," Carlton replied. "Man, keep pressing that damn button until that shit comes."

"What if everyone trying to get on at once and slowing this bitch down? What if everything shut down in this building? This damn elevator never takes this long. Man, we stuck in here with this crazy ass bitch," Calvin said now panicking.

"Good point, follow me," Carlton led the way to the kitchen and pulled open the drawer with the knives. He passed one to his brother and took on for himself. "Okay, we'll use these to protect ourselves while waiting on the elevator."

A swift breeze brushed passed both of them and knocked their phones to the ground. The sound of their phone being cracked on the marble floor caused the boys to freeze.

"What the hell was that?" Carlton asked.

"It's that crazy bitch. We're going to die man," Calvin panicked, while fighting back tears.

"No, we're not! This bitch can't be that fast and quick." Carlton looked around trying to spot her.

"Maybe our eyes can adjust to the dark over there by the window," Calvin whispered to his brother.

They both stood completely still when they heard footsteps approaching them. As the steps grew closer, they both swung their knives. They could feel their long knives go through tough skin and getting jammed. They tried to pull the knife out to stab her again, but couldn't.

"My fucking knife is stuck!" Calvin shouted.

"Mine is too," Carlton said. "Kick this bitch!"

Both of the boys raised their feet simultaneously and kicked Faith in the stomach, sending her flying backwards across the room.

"Let's finish this bitch off before she gets up," Carlton said, knowing Calvin would agree.

They have watched plenty of scary movies where the victim over powers the killer, but stop and start running before finishing the job. They ran into the living room near the floor to ceiling windows. The lights from the other buildings gave them enough light in the living room to see. When their eyes adjusted, they couldn't believe what they had done. Travis's body was lying there with both of their knives stuck inside of him. He was still squirming around, making moaning sounds.

"Oh shit! What the hell?" Calvin shouted, looking at him squirming on the floor with no arms and his head hanging to the side. The only thing that kept his head from falling off was a long bone in the center. "Lord, please, get us out of here!"

"I don't think the Lord is going to save you tonight," Faith said.

The boys turned to see her standing completely naked, covered in blood with a small axe in her hand and a strange smile on her face. As she stepped forward, they stepped backwards. Soon, she was standing right in front of Travis' body. "It amazes me that he is still alive and moving." She bent over and grabbed Travis' head with both hands and pulled hard on his head.

"Oh my God!" Calvin hollered as she ripped Travis' head completely from his body.

She pulled his head face to face to hers and could see Travis' eyes still moving, and then said, "Hmm, I wonder if your mind still works and if you know what's going on, even after your head has been decapitated from your body?" She looked over at the twins as if she was waiting for them to answer.

They both stood there frozen in fear. "If we stay by the window, we can see her coming and together, we can over power the crazy ass bitch. She can only cut one of us at a time. I'll take a chop if I have to and you rush her and knock her ass out," Carlton planned in a whisper.

Faith continued to smile as the boys whispered and rolled the head like a bowling ball. The boys looked down at their friend's head rolling on the smooth floor in front of them and stopped at their feet. They looked at Travis' face and he winked at them.

"Oh, hell no! Hell fucking no!" Calvin shouted, and then looked up to see Faith was gone. "I'm not with this shit, I'm gone!" he shouted.

"Don't panic, we need to stay together," Carlton said when he looked up to see Faith was out of sight too. He turned to look at his brother and Calvin took off running, "No Calvin! We need to stay by the window, so we can see her coming! Don't go into the dark!" Carlton shouted, but it was too late.

"I got to get out of here. I got to get out of here," Calvin repeated, "Lord, please save me," he panicked as he wandered around in the dark looking for the elevator.

"Didn't I tell you God wasn't going to save your ass tonight, boy?" He heard a voice whisper into his ear.

His body trembled in fear and snot began dripping out of his nose.

"Ahhhh!" he screamed when he felt Faith grab his legs from under him. He slammed to the floor chin first. Faith slammed the axe in the middle of his back, cutting through the skin all the way to the bone. She pulled the axe up and slammed it again, cracking his spine in half. Calvin tried to get up, but couldn't move his legs. Faith wrapped her arms around his legs and began to drag him.

Carlton stood by the window scared to move. He could hear his brother's screams loud and clear.

"Help me! Carlton, help me! I can't move my legs! No, no! Not my dick! Stop! Please, stop! Mommy! Mommy, help me! Carlton! Carlton, help me!"

Tears flowed down Carlton's chest from hearing his brother cry out for help. "I told you not to run, I told your ass to stay in the light," Carlton mumbled to himself, "What to do? I can't leave him." He walked to what was left of Travis' body and grabbed the handle to one of the knives jammed into his chest. He stepped on Travis' stomach while pulling and yanked the knife out.

"Help, Help!" Calvin cried hysterically.

Carlton's head ached and his stomach bubbled in fear, as he fought back the gassy feeling he had. He slowly walked over to his brother's cries, barely able to see his own hands in front of him. He stood close to his brother's screams, it started to die down and turned into grunting noises. He opened the bedroom door and entered the room.

"Help me," Calvin mumbled.

"I'm here, Calvin." His eyes began to adjust a little and he could see shapes and certain things. The floor was wet and sticky; he knew it was blood right away. He then noticed a hand, then an arm and leg; which still had a part of the jeans his brother had on attached to it. "No! No!" Carlton screamed and cried uncontrollably.

He walked toward the bed and saw his brother lying there with all of his limbs chopped off of his body. His body was cut in half at the waistline and he had a broomstick stuck up his asshole. Calvin moved around on the bed, flopping like a fish. Carlton stepped closer to his brother in shock, unable to make a noise, and touched his brother's head.

"Ahhh!" Calvin let out a weak scream.

He lifted his brother's head and dropped it, once he saw that his eyes had been dug out and his penis was stuck inside of his mouth. Carlton couldn't control his body as every inch began to shake and tears came flowing down his face.

He reached out and grabbed his brothers penis and pulled out of his mouth, "Run, run it's a trap!" Calvin spit out.

"Shh. I wont leave you," Carlton replied still crying.
Faith laid under the bed singing, "Yes, Jesus loves me. Yes, Jesus loves me. Yes, Jesus loves me, cause the bible tells me so."

Carlton panicked when he heard her voice and grabbed the knife tighter, while his body still trembled, trying to figure out where the voice was coming from, "Oh shit, under the bed. Faith swung with all her might, chopping off his left foot from the ankle.

"Ahhhhh!" Carlton screamed and began to hop away with pain traveling through his whole body. He looked back and could see his foot, still inside the new pair of Jordan's he had on and Faith crawling from up under the bed.

"Run, run," Calvin shouted out worried for his brother that he could not help or see.

The lights in the condo suddenly came back on. **Ding! Ding!** Carlton heard the elevator arrive. He continued to hop and look back, noticing the blood all over the floors and walls. He looked back to Faith slowly coming towards him, and he turned and looked forward.

"All I have to do is get pass the living room. The elevator is right there," he said. He smiled, seeing the elevator was just a few feet away. He looked back at Faith squatting down. "What the fuck is she doing?" he screamed out loud, "Oh shit!" he screamed as he realized what she was doing, but it was too late. Faith's axe cut through the air like a Frisbee and slammed into the back of his thigh. "Ahhhhahh!" he screamed and fell forward, face first to the floor. He began to crawl to the elevator as the door opened up. "I can make it, I can make it," he repeated.

"No you can't, fuck boy," Faith said and pulled the axe out of his thigh and chopped off his right arm, in one swift blow.

"Ahhh!" Carlton screamed again, but continued to crawl towards the elevator. "I can make it; I can make it."

"I already told you, boy, you're not going to make it. Hahaha, blame your damn daddy. He shouldn't play with a woman's heart," Faith said as she sat on his back, then pulled out her flip knife, raised it high, and came down hard.

"Ahhh! Lord! Lord help!" Carlton hollered. He could feel the knife rip open his skin and now Faith's hand was inside of him.

"Carlton, are you ok? Run, Carlton! Run and don't look back," "Calvin screamed.

She stuck her hand inside the wound she made and moved it around, pushing her arm deeper in until she felt organs. She stopped once she felt the beat, and wrapped her hand around his heart and yanked at it. Carlton's body went limp as she managed to pull his heart out.

"Hmm, that was fun," she said, staring at his heart in her hands,"

"Carlton, Carlton?" Alvin screamed for his brother while squirming around on the bed no longer hearing the screams of his brother.

"Hmm, I thought he would have bleed out by now. I guess I get to have more fun with him," she threw Carlton's heard on the floor and proceeded to the master bedroom where Calvin lay, "Yes, Jesus loves me. Yes, Jesus loves me. Yes, Jesus loves me, cause the bible tells me so,"

Calvin heard the singing getting closer and much more clearer, "Ahhhhh!" he screamed wishing the pain would end, but knowing this was only the beginning.

Chapter 12

Antonio woke up bright and early from the sounds of their two-year-old crying. He looked beside him and noticed that his wife wasn't laying next to him. Antonio got out of the bed and grabbed his robe. He walked out of the bedroom, down the stairs, and into the kitchen to see Sabrina and Veronica.

While feeding Veronica in the highchair, she turned to Antonio and said, "Hey, did you hear from the boys? I texted them last night, but didn't get a reply,"

"No, I just got up, but it's normal for them not to answer the phone when they're with their ghetto, rich friends," Antonio replied.

"Well, I hope so because I have a bad feeling. I hope they just dropped that crazy woman off. You can't keep doing this, Antonio. Can't you see the effect it has on your family? You have to learn to control yourself. You said there's nothing wrong with Veronica, but she hasn't stopped crying since that crazy woman kicked her. I think we should take her to the hospital," Sabrina stated.

"No, we can't do that. They're going to write a report and investigate. We don't need that and she's going to say a woman kicked her. She will be just fine," Antonio replied.

"No, the fuck she won't, Antonio. None of us will be just fine with you out here fucking bitches left and right, making them believe you love them. What, you can't get pussy without telling these bitches you love them?"

"That's not the case, baby. It's just a mind game, that's all. But these women don't love me, you do."

"Hmm, I'm starting to question my love for you. But that bitch loved you, you could see in her eyes that she believed every word you told her just like my foolish ass. You broke her heart! You can't keep doing that."

"Listen, I don't got time for this shit, fuck you!" Antonio shouted.

Sabrina looked around the kitchen and spotted the glass centerpiece in the middle of the kitchen table. She grabbed it and launched it at the back of Antonio's head with furious strength, causing him to fall forward and hit the floor, the glass shattering everywhere.

"Fuck me? Nigga, fuck me? I've been putting up with this shit for years! Women popping up, babies popping up, and I still stood beside you, holding your arm giving off the image that we had a perfect marriage and you got the nerve to say fuck me? You done brought this psycho bitch to our home, got our child harmed, and God knows where my sons are, and you look me in my face and say fuck me? Nah bitch, fuck you!" Sabrina shouted as she walked over to him, while he was rocking back and forth on the floor holding his head, trying to stop the bleeding, "Fuck this marriage too," she said as she snatched her ring off and threw it on top of him. "Now, get the fuck out of my house!"

Antonio staggered to his feet still holding the back of his head. He looked at his wife walking back to their daughter and wanted to say something, but knew he put his foot in his mouth. He went upstairs as fast as he could, got dressed, and left.

Chapter 13

Faith sat in the 2015 black Cadillac Escalade with the keys she took from Carlton's pocket. She grabbed the jar in the passenger seat, which held four different sizes, shapes, and colors of all four of the boys' penises.

"Bet you won't rape anyone else." She placed the jar back on the passenger seat, next to the bigger jar that was filled with water and Travis' decapitated head.

She laid back in the seat and watched as Antonio's green Mercedes Benz pulled out of the garage, and then, out of the driveway. Faith watched the car disappear down the road, and then she started the truck and drove up the driveway of their two story home. She looked up on the sun visor and was happy to see the garage door opener. She pushed the button and watched the door rise and she slowly drove in.

"Oh, it sounds like your brothers are finally home," Sabrina said to her daughter and scooped her up into her arms, walking to the garage door by the kitchen. She opened the door to see her sons' truck pulled in. "Why the fuck y'all wasn't answering the phone?"

The tinted windows on the truck made it impossible to see in the truck. Faith grabbed Calvin's head out of the backseat, hopped out of the truck and tossed the skull like a baseball. The head crashed into Sabrina's forehead like a head-butt. She stumbled backwards as blood dripped down her face from the new, fresh wound and a speed knot grew on her head that began to throb. She did her best not to fall, knowing she had Veronica in her arms. Something told her to look down to see what hit her and she looked in despair.

"Aahhhh!" she screamed at the top of her lungs when she realized she was hit with her son's head, with the eyes dug out of the skull.

Faith calmly walked over to Sabrina and bent down. She stuck her index finger and her ring finger in the eye sockets of the head like a bowling ball and swung, hitting Sabrina in her left temple. This time, she couldn't control her body from falling and collapsed onto the kitchen floor, briefly losing consciousness.

"Auuh, ugh," she groaned in pain. The sound of running water and her daughter could be heard. She felt like this was all a dream and her head was pounding terribly. She opened her eyes to see that she was still in the kitchen, *'God, please let this all be a bad dream.'* She tried to move, but she looked down and saw that she was tied up with sheets, wrapped around the kitchen chair. She tried to scream but couldn't.

Faith entered the room holding Veronica, while she was crying, trying to break free. "I see you like to scream, so I found some old period panties and stuffed them in your mouth."

Sabrina heard a whimpering sound and Faith walked over to take the panties out of her mouth. Sabrina cried uncontrollably and said so many things at once, she could barely be understood.

"If you calm your pretty little head, maybe I can understand you, dear," Faith said in a nonchalantly tone.

Sabrina took a deep breath. "Why did you do that to my son? Where is Carlton?"

"Your sons have, I mean had, my mistake. Hahaha! Your sons seemed to have inherited the same problem as their father with their dicks. The little horny shits and their friends took me to the condo and raped me! Let's just say, they all got fucked back," Faith explained. Sabrina cried a silent cry and her heart went numb, thinking of what she had done to her children. "Anything else?" Faith asked.

"Please, don't hurt us, just please put my daughter down. Where is my dog? I can hear her crying?" Sabrina asked, while crying. Faith just stood there smiling like the Grinch that stole Christmas. "Muffin! Come here, Muffin girl," she screamed out to her Pomeranian.

Muffin slowly slid in the kitchen from the living room and

inched her way to Sabrina's legs. Sabrina looked in horror, looking at Muffin with her forelegs cut off. The little parts that were left was wrapped up in white gauze with blood seeping through.

"What did you do to my dog, you crazy bitch?" Sabrina shouted.

Faith raised her right eyebrow. "Really bitch? I'm standing here dangling your damn nappy head ass daughter. I killed your lil dick having ass sons and you're yelling at me about a damn dog? If you must know, the bitch was driving me crazy. It wasn't so much the barking; it was those little feet tapping around on the damn floor. It sounded like she has on damn tapping shoes. I couldn't take that shit no more, so I cut her damn feet off... there. You happy?" Faith walked off and came back with one of the dog's legs. "Here girl, come get it. Come get it girl." She waved the leg at the dog, making kissing sounds over by Sabrina's legs, causing Muffin to slide to her, grabbing the leg and eating it. "The funny part is, the bitch even eats the bone. That's what she did to the first one. I wonder do she know that it's her leg? Hmm, guess we'll never know. Oh, and don't worry, she's not in any pain. I went into the medicine cabinet upstairs, found a great stash that I'm sure your husband isn't supposed to have and shot her ass up with some morphine."

"You sick, stupid bitch! All of this because my husband doesn't want you. You doing this because one measly man don't want you. Fuck you!" Sabrina shouted like a crazy woman.

"Hmm, it seems as though you forget who has the upper hand here," Faith said while bouncing Veronica up and down in her arms.

"You wouldn't. I'm sorry, I take it back," Sabrina said while crying.

Faith smiled and picked the bloody panties off the table and stuffed them back in her mouth. She tilted and dragged the chair Sabrina was tied to across the kitchen, passed the living room, and into the guest bathroom on the first floor. The floor was over flooded with water as the bathtub was left running. Faith placed Sabrina in front of the bathtub.

"No, this isn't over a man. This is just who I am. Antonio was the reason I wouldn't allow myself to be this person; the person my father said was already in me. I guess he was right because this shit feels better than sex. Hurting people, seeing them cry and scream, gives me a weird type of high. I can't explain it. It covers up the pain your husband put me through. Having me think he cared for me and loved me, was the worst mistake he ever made. So, for the pain I felt, I'm going to hurt him ten times more. It seems as the only thing he loves more than himself is his children. I mean, you heard that little speech he gave me yesterday. If I could remember properly, I believe you laughed and taunted me about how he broke my heart. Well, let's see if I can get another laugh out of you," Faith said, while smiling like something was mentally wrong with her.

Sabrina quickly caught on to what was about to happen next. "No! No!" she mumbled through the panties and rocked her chair back and forth.

"Mommy! Mommy!" Veronica cried out from seeing the panic and tears in her mother's eyes and tried to wiggle away.

Faith sat on the edge of the bathtub and looked at Sabrina. "Yesterday, you asked how much would it be to get rid of me. At that time, I didn't know the price, but now I do. It's your family's lives. That's my price," Faith said as she tossed the two-year-old baby in the bathtub and held her head under the water. Veronica kicked and scratched at Faith to break free.

Sabrina screamed and rocked the chair trying to get loose. Her mouth was so soaked from the screaming, she had to try not to choke on her own saliva. Tears poured out of her eyes as she watched her daughter fight for her life, knowing she couldn't help her. The bubbles eventually stopped rising to the top of the tub water and the splashing stopped.

"I guess it's over. The funny thing is, this child put up a better fight than all of you." Faith pulled Veronica's body out of the tub and hung it over the tub like a wet towel.

"Ahhhahhahh!" Sabrina cried hysterically.

Faith removed the small axe from her waist and wiped Sabrina's tears away with it. "Wait, the best part isn't done yet." She walked back to Veronica's body, grabbed her by the hair, and swung the axe through her neck. The axe ripped through her neck, taking her head all the way off. Sabrina managed to push the panties out of her mouth and screamed from the top of her lungs. Faith dropped Veronica's head and walked back over to Sabrina.

"Don't you wish you would have chosen a better man; a non-cheating scumbag?" Faith asked and swung her axe. She looked confused when she felt her axe being blocked. She looked and saw her axe crossed up with a machete. Faith was now face to face with Black Ice.

"I see you have more than a little bit of me in you, my child," Black Ice said while laughing, "Hahahaha!" His laugh sent chills through Sabrina and Faith's body.

Faith tried not to show it, but it was something about her father that she couldn't help, but fear. "Yes, daddy, I'm just like you. Are you happy now? So, let me finish this bitch in peace," she said, while pulling her axe back.

"You're a far cry from being just like me. You're still sloppy and have a lot to learn. Besides, you still fear me, bitch. You're not ready until you fear nothing, not even the devil. And you're not killing her."

"What the fuck you mean I'm not killer her?" Faith shouted.

death. She's coming with us and she's mine now. Daddy is going to have a little fun with her."

Flashbacks of the first time she seen a woman gutted alive like a pig played in her mind. She smiled, knowing her father was right. Death was easy, but life was hard.

"Okay," she replied.

"Good. Gather your souvenirs, we got to go."

Faith reached down and grabbed Veronica's head and ran back to the front to grab the dog and Calvin's head.

Sabrina couldn't believe what she saw nor what she was hearing. This tall strange man in her house was this crazy bitch's father. Black Ice stood in front of her and Sabrina looked at him strangely. He was tall, dark, and handsome. He looked as if he lived in the gym and had a long scar across his face. The only way you could tell he was a killer was by his eyes, voice, and demeanor. He smiled and kissed her on the forehead. His lips were soft, wet, and comforting.

He broke the embrace. "You're my bitch now!" he shouted and swung, punching her in the side of her head. All she could see were stars before losing consciousness.

Chapter 14

Antonio rode the elevator up, reaching two floors away from reaching his penthouse. "I can't wait until this is all over. I'm throwing all that bitch's shit away. Well, maybe not all of it, I paid good money for all that name brand shit. I can save it and keep it for the next bitch, she won't know the difference." He joked around in the elevator, still holding his wound from his wife in the back of his head. "Then again, I may just throw everything away.

The elevator door opened and his heart and jaw dropped. Blood was everywhere, like a massacre had taken place in his condo. In front of the elevator was a headless body with a missing arm and a leg. Antonio pulled out his .45 from his blue blazer and his IPhone to call 911, but before he could start the call, he dropped his phone and to his knees in tears, recognizing that it was his son's body.

"No, no, no!" he shouted, while crying. He stayed there for ten minutes in shock, and then searched the rest of the condo, where he found his other son on the bed with all of his limbs chopped off. He recognized them from the clothes that they were wearing, "Why?" he asked, while looking up. "Oh shit, Sabrina and Veronica!"

Antonio tried to call his wife, but didn't get an answer, so he called the police and explained that someone may be trying to kill his wife. He rushed out of the condo and was in his car in a blink of an eye, driving as fast as he could through every stop sign and red light. He was shocked to see that he beat the police home. He parked in front and pulled out his gun before he entered the house.

With his gun leading the way into the house, he called out, "Sabrina! Veronica!" he shouted, but no answer.

The first thing he noticed was the puddle of water on the floor and could hear running water from the tub. He entered the kitchen first to see Muffin dead, lying on the kitchen floor with no legs.

"Sabrina? Baby?" he shouted once more, and then heard his phone ringing. The call was from his wife and his heart began to beat slowly. He answered, "Hey baby, where are you and Veronica? I'm worried," he asked, praying she was out shopping.

"And you should be." He heard a voice and his heart sank when he recognized it was Faith.

"Bitch, you killed my sons! I'm going to fucking kill you, I swear, you bitch!" Antonio said while crying.

Faith could hear the pain in his voice and it brought joy to her. "I bet you'll think twice before you play with another woman's heart, before you tell someone else you love them and don't mean it. You broke my heart, Antonio," Faith said sinisterly.

"Fuck you! I never loved you, you were just good pussy. I used you! I'm going to kill your black ass, bitch! I promise you I'm going to kill you!" he screamed with spit flying out of his mouth and tears all over his face.

"I see you and your wife have a lot in common; you both tend to forget who has the upper hand."

Antonio pulled the phone from his ear and looked at the screen to see his wife's name. For a second, he forgot she had called him from his wife's phone.

"Where's my wife and my daughter, hoe?" he shouted after putting the phone back up to his ear.

"You still think you're in control, huh Antonio? You're the hoe. Remember this, you male hoe, if you were faithful to your wife, none of this would have happened. If you didn't hurt me and break my heart, I wouldn't be the way that I am now," Faith replied.

"Fuck your heart, bitch. Where is my family?"

"Fuck my heart? Fuck my heart?" she repeated and her anger raised, "Go to your guest bathroom, Antonio," Faith said and stayed on the phone quietly, tapping her feet while she waited.

Antonio stepped into the water and made his way to the guest room. He looked down and could see water was getting deeper. He squeezed the grip on his gun tightly. "Please, just jump out on me bitch, so I can empty this whole damn clip on your ass," he mumbled.

"You won't be that lucky, baby," she replied as she twirled her axe in her hand.

Antonio walked into the bathroom and noticed that the water was different; it was much darker and mixed with blood. His eyes opened wide, "NO, NO, NO!" his tears flooded like a river looking at his daughter's body in a red and black polka dot dress, slouched over the bathtub without her head attached. "NOOOO!" he ran over to her body and picked it up, pulling it closer to his chest. "Lord why? Noooo! God nooo!" he screamed, while crying and rocking back and forth.

"You broke my heart, so I broke you. Oh, I have everyone's head. Hahahahaha!"

Antonio could hear Faith talking and laughing before he dropped his phone in the water. "No, no, no, no!" He sat there on his knees, holding his daughter tightly.

Excerpt of...
THE DAUGHTER OF BLACK ICE 2

Faith stared at Black Ice as he drove the van. She looked out of the passenger side window into the rearview mirror and could see the other vans following close behind.

"Where are we going?" she asked.

Black Ice turned his head and looked back at her, "You've earned the right to ask me two questions, only two, until you can prove yourself to me even more," he responded with a smirk on his face.

"Ok, my first question is, where the hell are we going?"

"For a young woman that has been locked in a shitty apartment most of your life, I'd think you'd be excited to see most of the world. But to answer your question, we are headed south, so that I can start training you. You're good, but no match for someone that has been killing longer than you," he answered.

"Train me for what? I think I'm a pretty good killer," she replied.

Black Ice had to fight the urge to laugh. "My child, you're okay, but remember, anybody can be a gorilla in a room full of chimpanzees. The question is can you be a gorilla in a room with a gorilla? Can you still be a wolf when more wolves are around? Can you be a killer amongst other killers? I don't think so, not yet. And I'm training you to help me kill your older sister and your two brothers, whom are better killers than you for the moment. But, you'll have me as a personal trainer, unlike them," Black Ice replied.

"Wait, what? Kill my brothers and sisters? Why? And why did my mother hate me so much?" Faith asked.

"Bitch, I told you, you had two questions. You have to earn the rest," he stated.

"Uggh!" Sabrina moaned. Her skull felt like it was cracked opened. She opened her eyes to see that she was in a moving van, "Help! Help!" she shouted.

Black Ice looked at Faith. "Can you handle that?"

"You should have just let me kill her. I wish I can kill Antonio, too," she said as she stood up and walked to the back of the van.

"Oh, you'll get your chance. He'll come looking for you with everything he's got," Black Ice warned her.

"Good," she replied, raising her leg and stomping back down on Sabrina's head, knocking her back out.

****

Regina walked fast and continued to look behind her. She was now in the state of Virginia and had been moving from state to state for the past eight months. She had been on the run ever since she laid eyes on Black Ice for the first time in twenty years. The only thing that slowed her down from staying on track was her urge to get high.

"Okay, I must get enough crack to last me, and then, I can find a small town and hide. He's never in small towns since he's so used to hiding in plain sight in cities I'd never go back to. I won't go back," she said as her mind flashed back to being trapped in a warehouse and women screaming as hyenas ripped through them, eating their flesh, "No, I won't go back," Regina repeated and turned down a block, "Okay, after I get this shit, I'll jump on a Greyhound out of this state and keep moving, so he won't find me," Regina said to herself and turned down an alley, still looking behind her.

She could see a young man with a fitted cap on dressed in all blue. She recognized him as Rome, the neighborhood drug dealer. She bought crack off of him for the past three weeks, but now, it was time to get enough to leave.

"Yo, Rome! I hope you got what I asked for. I don't have time for no small dime bags," she said, but he didn't answer or move.

His back was leaned against the wall and his left leg was posted on the wall, as if he was about to take a picture. She moved closer and touched his shoulder and as soon as she did, Rome's head fell off of his body and rolled a few inches away.

"No, no, no. Not again. I won't go back, you hear me," Regina pulled out a chrome 380 handgun from her bra and squeezed the trigger, firing wild in the narrow alley. Bullets hit brick walls and ricocheted everywhere, "I'm not going back, you hear me!" she shouted, and then stopped shooting and raised the gun to her temple. Her finger twitched as she prepared to pull the trigger. "I can't let him get me," she mumbled, knowing that death would be a lot better than what Black Ice would do to her.

She could hear something fast cutting through the air. She squinted her eyes and could see a small axe flying towards her, but it was too late to react. The axe ripped through her flesh and cut off her hand that was holding the gun.

"Ahhhhh! No, I won't go back!" she hollered in pain and bent over to try to get the gun from her now, detached right hand.

She saw someone kick the hand away and send a blow to her face. Once she opened her eyes, she saw Faith standing over her, but she wasn't the same girl she raised. She seemed stronger and darker.

"Hello, mother. Now, I can't have you killing yourself, that would be such an easy way out. Plus, my father has plans for you," Faith said with an evil smile on her face.

"No, I won't go back!" Regina shouted.

"Yes, you are, bitch." Regina heard a deep demonic voice and knew who it belonged to.

Regina was roughly grabbed by the collar of her shirt, dragged backwards to the van and tossed inside.

"Your mine, bitch," Black Ice said before he locked the back of the van.

Regina held her right arm while screaming, "Noooo! Not again! Nooo!"

**More releases by True Glory
Publications. Just click the Link!**
Shameek Speight

Child of a Crackhead

Child of a Crackhead II

Pleasure of Pain

Ink Mistress

Unfaithful: A Tale of a Broken Marriage

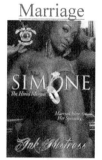

Simone: The Hired Mistress

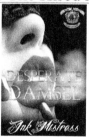

Desperate Damsel

Marques Lewis

The Woman That Got Away

CoCo Dior

PRINCESS IN THE TRAP

Melikia Gaino

FALLING FOR A DRUG DEALER

WHO'S GOING TO LOVE YOU BUT ME

Adrian Thomas

MONEY ID THE MOTIVE

CPSIA information can be obtained
at www.ICGtesting.com
Printed in the USA
LVOW04s1737021216
515533LV00009B/540/P